Crushes

Crushes

Stories

Eric Shay Howard

I've been writing on these a few a year for a long time, but like a crush, after a while I couldn't really tell you when any of them started or if any of them are done.

Contents

He Built A Birdhouse

There was a knock at the door thirty minutes into dinner. Abigail was the quickest to her feet. She walked from the kitchen table and opened the front door. A short brown-haired man was standing outside. He wore dark dress pants and a white dress shirt with dirt near his heart. He held a large duffel bag over his shoulder. Sweat dripped from his forehead.

"Hello, my name's Jack. I'm looking for Mr. Colt. I'd like to ask him if I could paint the birds." Abigail turned her head to the table and looked at her dad. Sheryl was sitting next to him, feeding him greens. Abigail smelled vinegar as she stood there in doorway.

"You want to paint the birds?" Abigail said.

"I'm an artist," Jack shook his black duffel bag. "I promise I won't hurt them."

"What is it, hon?" Sheryl stood up from the table.

Abigail walked back to the table, around Sheryl, and kissed her dad on his head. His one lock of hair tickled her cheek.

"I'll be back." Abigail put her plate of country-fried steak, mashed potatoes, and greens on the top shelf of the refrigerator, uncovered, scooting the tea in the milk jug further to the back with the edge of the plate. Abigail felt Sheryl watching her from the table until she stepped out onto the front porch. Three elephant ears in red clay pots blocked the view of the singing windchimes from the trailer next door.

"Can you follow me in my truck?" Abigail said.

"Sorry, I walked." Jack turned the elbow on his arm holding the duffel bag in towards his waist.

Abigail walked down the wooden steps and walked around to the back, past the rusted triangular hook on the side of the trailer that had never been removed and on past the missing piece of the underpinning. Jack followed her to her green ninety-nine Toyota parked at the end of the backyard down by the hayfield. She unlocked the driver's side and got in. She tapped the window on the passenger's side. Jack got in, then she scratched her nose and drove down a path in the middle of the overgrown grass behind the trailers.

"How'd you know about the birds?" Abigail asked.

"I read about them in one of the journals. I forget the name." They got out of the truck at a wooden fence that came up to Jack's elbows. Abigail stretched her legs over it one by one. Jack did the same. Abigail grabbed his bicep when his bag fell and the paintbrushes scattered on the ground.

"My dad never built the gate for it." She helped him down.

"It alright if I feed 'em?" Jack asked. He knelt and stayed down for a moment before he pulled out a small plastic bag of bird seed from his duffel, Wild Delight, the expensive stuff.

"Alright. Watch your step." It had been nearly a month since Abigail had been out this way. After a bit of cautious footing, they came up on a few empty dark brown nests. Abigail saw a few rusty blackbirds pecking at the dirt through the weeds. A large wooden box was on the ground.

"Is that their birdhouse?" Jack said.

"My dad made it for them. There's another one a ways that way," She pointed forward. "He was gonna build another one but they don't use them much. You're welcome to paint them," Abigail said. She stepped over a cocklebur.

"No, the wood looks better this way," Jack said. Yellow purslane marked the spot before the bird population became the densest. Abigail stopped at the crescendo of flailing wings and whistles. Jack squatted, opened his bag of bird seed, stuck his hand in, and lifted out a mound of seed with his palm. Twenty or so birds twitched and darted over. Jack pulled his hand away and stood back up, dropping the seed to the ground. He clenched his fist and watched the birds as they pecked at the seeds.

"What journal did you say you were doing this for?" Abigail asked.

"I'm just a freelance artist." He folded up the bird seed and walked back towards his duffel bag. He pulled out a sketchbook, then walked back over and sat down near the remains of the bird seed. Abigail brought a bird over to Jack.

"See the wings?" She held the bird out to him. The lead in his pencil scratched against his paper and he nodded. Abigail sat the bird down and it strutted back over to the other birds it had been taken from. Jack flinched when a small bird brushed up against him.

"I can't stay out here long," Abigail said.

"Don't mind me," Jack said. The bird that had startled him stepped away.

"Are you okay getting back?" Abigail asked.

Jack nodded and continued to sketch. Abigail watched him for a few more minutes and smiled after a thought as she walked back to the fence, hopped it, and got in her car. She drove back later that evening to check on Jack, but he was already gone. Later that night, Abigail's dad was being very ornery. He refused to take off his Wrangler jeans and wouldn't take a bath.

"It ain't your job to do this, hon. Go on to bed," Sheryl told Abigail. Sheryl was very attentive to Abigail's dad, even more so after Sheryl divorced him five years ago, right before the Alzheimer's started to really kick in. She bought the trailer across the road, but then she all but moved back in to help take care of him when Abigail left for college.

A gun fired.

Abigail flipped on the porch light and stepped onto the back porch. A bullet plowed into the garden in the back yard next door. A man wailed before he hit the ground. Abigail ran towards her mother's trailer across the property line. Her mother was in a white nightgown and barefoot, holding a rifle in both hands, looking through the scope and walking towards the garden.

"Abby, there's somebody back here," Abigail's mom said.

"Put the gun down, Mom." Abigail recognized the duffel bag on the ground. "Jack, can you get up? Mom, help me get him to my car."

Jack lifted his hand from his shoulder. The top of his shoulder was bleeding. The wound was long and thin, like a cut from a knife.

"Just grazed it." Abigail's mom said.

"I came back the wrong way," Jack said.

A baby bird chirped. It was wrapped inside Jack's

right hand. Jack let go of the bird, but the bird didn't leave his hand. He breathed in and wiggled his palm out from under the bird. Jack let go of his breath when the bird took a step.

"I found him in my bag. I was gonna take him back."

"Don't leave that damn bird here." Abigail's mom pointed her rifle. Jack picked the bird up. Abigail's mom walked up her three concrete steps underneath her back door and went back inside her trailer. No light shined out of the windows.

"Come on." Abigail picked up Jack's bag and he stood up. "Get in my car. I'll drive you to the hospital."

"No, I think I'm fine, really. The bullet's not in there." Abigail vaguely remembered seeing something in the garden splatter when the gun went off.

"You gonna introduce me?" Sheryl was standing out on the back porch as Abigail stepped over into her dad's yard.

"Jack, this is Sheryl. Sheryl, Jack. He's a friend from school." Jack looked at Abigail. He clutched the bird in his right hand and held out his left as he turned back toward Sheryl. Sheryl smiled and touched his hand, but removed it quickly.

"You might as well let him stay the night, then. Make sure his arm don't fall off."

"No, I couldn't."

"You got a family to get back to?"

"No ma'am."

"Then I insist. Hell, you pissed off Madeline. You earned it." Sheryl patted Jack's shoulder. When they got inside, Abigail checked Jack under the light.

"Don't even think it needs stitches." Abigail pressed a wet rag against his shoulder.

"You a doctor?"

"No. I'm an anthropologist."

"You don't strike me as an Anthropology kind of girl."

"Jack, you like onions?" Sheryl laid out some blankets along the couch.

"Yes ma'am."

"Good. I'll make us a good brunch tomorrow. We're not really breakfast people but help yourself in the morning if you want." Sheryl patted the blankets, then went into the hall and grabbed a cardboard box from a shelf above the washer and dryer space. "Put that bird in here."

Jack obeyed. Sheryl tossed a pillow on the couch. Abigail wrapped up Jack's shoulder with a white cloth and then went into her dad's room. Her dad had fallen asleep in his jeans sitting up in bed. She laid him down gently and then went into her own bedroom and closed the door. She got undressed and turned her stereo on low. It just barely fit on top of the dresser by the door. She had to hold onto the left speaker to flip the light switch behind it. An old country song that she didn't remember the name of played on the radio. She flipped the disc changer and "I Forgive But I Won't Forget" by Lacuna Coil came on as she got into bed. Her right leg hung out from under the sheet. The blanket was coiled up against a window that looked out into the front yard. She looked through her window and on past Sheryl's rusted white truck outside, and on through the front windows of the trailer across the street. Abigail could see Sheryl's old cuckoo clock against the back wall through one of the windows, and she could see stacks of boxes in the kitchen. Abigail remembered when the clock was over here, and then she remembered the day Sheryl moved it over there. Then she remembered her dad before she'd left for college. Then Jack's face came up, his mouth curved into something like a smile.

Abigail awoke and looked over at the green digits on her stereo. It was two minutes past ten. She smelled onions. She put on yesterday's jeans and walked to the little bathroom in the hall. The door was locked. The shower was running. Her dad was sitting in his recliner in the living room watching the news. Sheryl was at the stove. The bird was in its box by the front door. The blankets and pillow were no longer on the couch. Abigail kissed her dad on the head and then poured herself a mug of coffee, black with a teaspoon of sugar, and sat down at the kitchen table.

"Did Karl show up and start cutting?" Abigail asked.

"You see anybody out there?" Sheryl asked.

"Just as well. Ya'll can't afford to keep paying him." Abigail flipped through a black binder at the kitchen table.

"Get your nose outa that business." Sheryl patted the binder closed and slipped the binder in a drawer under the island between the kitchen and the living room. Jack came down the hallway. He wore a white t-shirt and a pair of maroon sweatpants. "Well, look at that." Sheryl smiled. Jack's face was overtaken by stubble. The cloth around his arm was gone. "It's almost ready." Sheryl turned the last burner off and let the potatoes crisp in the pan while she grabbed the plates out of the cabinet above the sink. Abigail's dad got up from his recliner and sat at the kitchen table in the chair closest to the living room. Abigail sat in the seat in front of the window. Sheryl squeezed into the chair on the back end of the table, up against a white china cabinet.

"These potatoes taste like shit," Henry said.

"Henry, that's an onion," Sheryl said.

"I don't want it!"

"Well give it here, then." Sheryl stabbed the onion with her fork, lifted it off his plate, and dropped it onto her own. "So, Jack, what color you paintin' those birds?" Jack looked up and opened his eyes wide at Abigail. He sat in the chair in front of the stove.

"She's joking," Abigail said. Sheryl laughed and Jack huffed out a chuckle.

"I was wondering if you wouldn't care if I painted again today?" Jack asked.

"You a art student, Jack?" Sheryl stared.

"Yes." He mashed food into his mouth. Sheryl's eyes were glued to his every move, every chew, every nibble. Henry started laughing at something, then he stood up, walked over to Abigail, and put his arms around her. Abigail let him hug and laugh at her for as long as he wanted. Sheryl got up from the table.

"I'll get the dishes after you're done. And your clothes are in the wash." Sheryl said both things looking straight at Jack, then she walked Henry into the back bedroom and closed the door behind her.

"So, is it okay if I stay and pant some more?" Jack asked.

"We can go back out there after you're done eating," Abigail said. Jack stood and picked up his plate. "No, don't." Abigail scooted her chair out and Jack sat his plate back down. She put on her tennis shoes and grabbed her keys off the top of her stereo in her room.

Jack picked up his bag and grabbed the bird out of the box before they left out the back door. Abigail drove them down the path. She held the baby bird for Jack while he came over the fence, managing to look like he'd done it before. He set up his easel and threw out a few handfuls of bird seed. The baby bird stayed right by Jack the entire time that he painted. It pecked on the back of Jack's foot; he tried to sidestep it but lost his balance and drew a line of blue all the way up the middle of the painting as he fell. He jumped back up.

"Is that watercolor?" Abigail said. Jack had painted a picture of a birdhouse.

"Yeah, why?"

"You just don't strike me as a watercolor kind of guy."

"What kind of guy do I strike you as?"

Abigail thought for a moment. "Oil pastels."

"Good God."

Abigail laughed.

The pitter-patter of a nearly shot muffler startled the birds. Sheryl climbed over the fence and ran over to them.

"Abby, I can't find Henry. I was takin' a bath and I came out and he was gone." Sheryl breathed in.

"I'll check over at Mom's."

"I called. She says he ain't over there. I'll check the barn." Sheryl breathed out.

"Call Karl."

"Got your phone?" Sheryl asked. Abigail put the password in her iPhone and handed it over. Sheryl waved her hands over the screen. Abigail took the phone back. "What's the number?"

"Three nines and a six." Abigail pushed the numbers and passed the phone back over to Sheryl. Sheryl held the phone high up over her ear, turning her head sideways. Abigail went back to her truck. Jack toppled over the fence without his bag. Abigail turned the truck around and lowered the driver's side window.

"You can stay here."

"I can help." Jack stood still.

"It's okay. He's probably out in the barn again." The window went up.

Sheryl climbed back over the fence, returned to her own truck, and drove it along the path towards the barn. Abigail turned a donut and drove back towards the trailer. She watched Jack stand with his feet together, his white shirt contrasting against the fence, until he was gone. She yelled for her dad. She turned the truck off and yelled through the missing underpinning. She went through the back door of the trailer to cool down and came out the front.

Abigail's mom was outside on the front porch of the trailer next door behind the elephant ears, her hands above her eyes, looking out into the wooded area behind the trailer across the road. After a few minutes she turned away, walked across the porch, and stared out the other side towards Lexington Avenue.

Karl's red four-door pickup truck came around the curve and passed the trailer. He came back about five minutes later and pulled into the driveway out front.

"I checked on down the hill. Didn't see 'em," Karl said after he stepped out. His brown boots crunched the rocks under his feet. His jeans were fitted, tucked into his boots, and his yellow collared shirt was tucked under his belt. He wore a new black leather hat that Abigail had never seen on him before. His black and silver hair poked out behind his ears.

"Sheryl went to the barn," Abigail said. Karl pointed with his thumb to the passenger side of the truck. Abigail shook her head and went back to her own truck in the backyard. Her mom was already standing with her back door open, looking out over the fields.

Abigail let Karl start down the path towards the barn and she followed. Abigail slowed down as she got closer to the fence that enclosed the birds and Karl drove on ahead. She got out and peaked over the fence; Jack wasn't there. She drove on down the path. She kept her eyes out over the grass and yelled for her dad until she got to the barn. Sheryl was standing outside the barn with one of her hands pointed towards it and the other on her waist. Both Karl and Sheryl turned their heads towards Abigail's truck when she pulled up to them.

"What happened to the barn door?" Abigail said.

"Hell if I know." Sheryl shook her head and raised her hands. Half of the barn door had been stripped off.

"Somebody pried out the nails. Look," Karl said. He

ran his hands down the wood.

They abandoned the path and searched out in the grass acre by acre. By the time the sun had set, the heavy trucks they all drove had nearly flattened the field. In the dark, they got out the flashlights and searched on foot. Abigail cut a breath short when her flashlight shined on Jack standing outside the fence, still in the maroon sweats that Sheryl gave him.

"I found him," Jack said. He climbed over the fence. Abigail dropped the flashlight as she went over. She picked it up as she ran through the birds and they fluttered and chirped and sang as she ran after Jack. "I can't lift him," Jack said after she caught up to him. A hammer and half a barn door were on the ground up next to Henry, who lay in the purslane. Abigail tried to lift him. Even with Jack's help, he was too heavy.

"Stay here. Don't leave." Abigail ran forward and hopped over the fence. She ran into the grass towards the barn. Karl's truck was there and he was sitting on the few square bales of hay left in the barn. "Karl, he's over here!" Abigail didn't want to stop running even though her throat felt like it was being cut with every breath that went down it. Karl pulled up beside her in the truck, but Abigail kept running until she choked on her slobber and had to stop to catch her breath. The door opened and she climbed up into the seat. He started driving before she got the door shut. "Over the fence." Abigail pointed and he sped up and hit the brakes just before the fence appeared in front of them. Abigail jumped out and ran with her flashlight until she found Jack. Karl was slow to catch up.

"Get his feet for me," Karl said. Jack grabbed Henry's ankles and they carried him over the fence and into Karl's truck. They laid him down in the narrow back seat of the four-door and closed the little door.

"You ride with him," Abigail said to Jack, pointing to Karl. Abigail turned and went to her own truck. She started it up and drove around in the field until she saw another light. Sheryl was walking along the grass that had already been driven through. "Sheryl, Karl's got him. He's on the way out."

"I'll ride with you," Sheryl said. Abigail drove them out of the field. She turned left onto the road, went on around the curve, and sped until she caught up with Karl's truck just before he turned onto Lexington Avenue.

Jack helped Karl pull Henry out of the backseat of the truck and they lugged him in through the electronic doors at the University of Kentucky hospital emergency entrance. Karl yelled. It took a long time for someone to bring out a stretcher. They laid Henry up on it and doctors rolled him away. Abigail took some forms from a red-haired man while Sheryl explained to the nurses what the matter was. Sheryl called Jack over and he told them something. Abigail finished the paperwork and sat in one of the cushioned chairs in the waiting room. She wrapped her arms around her legs in the chair with her hands locked together. Sheryl and Jack came back and sat beside her. Karl sat across from them.

"It's late Karl. You've done more than enough. Why don't ya head on out. We'll let ya know about Henry," Sheryl said. Karl put his hat back on over his two puffs of gray hair.

"Ya'll gonna be alright to drive back?"

"I reckon Jack can drive us back in Abby's truck if need be," Sheryl said.

"Yes ma'am," Jack said.

"Alright. Let me know," Karl said. He left out the double doors and turned left towards the snack machine.

"So ya found 'em with the birds? How ya reckon he got that door from all the waydatha barn? You see anything?" Sheryl asked. She looked at Jack.

"Well I was just painting and I heard something just before dark. I walked over to check it out and it looked like the fence fell."

"Before dark? How long was he layin' there?" Jack sucked his lower lip into his mouth. "Don't look at her, look at me."

"I went back to painting for a while. Maybe an hour. I went over there again and saw him. And I couldn't find any of you until Abigail came back over." Sheryl slowly started to nod to herself. "I'd like to paint the birds some more. It looks like you need help on the farm. I can work."

"Colt?" A doctor came out of a room down the hall past a desk with a heart-shaped lamp on the back edge. Abigail put her feet on the ground but Sheryl pointed at her. Abigail stayed seated and Sheryl followed the doctor. Sheryl came back and got Abigail a while later and took her to the room where Henry was sleeping. His skin was yellow. Abigail sat in the room with Sheryl and they watched Here Comes Honey-Boo-Boo on the little widescreen that was mounted on the wall.

The next morning, Doctor Andrews said Henry's liver was starting to shut down. They found Melanoma in his bloodstream and it had spread to his other organs. By that evening, plans were made to get Hospice to come out to the trailer. Sheryl just kept telling Henry that he was getting to go home soon.

"You still wanna paint them birds?" Sheryl asked Jack.

"Yes I do," Jack said.

"Alright." She handed him a set of keys. "To the trailer across the street. It's still got some stuff stored in there, but I reckon we can move most of it over and you can stay there while you're workin'." Jack took the keys, crammed his whole hand inside his right pocket before letting go of them, and then tapped his sweats. He drove

Sheryl and Abigail home. Hospice helped Sheryl arrange Henry's room the next day.

Karl showed Jack how to cut the hay.

"It's just like mowing the yard. First you use this one, then you go over it all again with this one, and then this one." Karl pointed at three detachable contraptions in the back of the barn next to the John Deere. Abigail watched Jack ride the tractor up and down the field. The black tarp hid the violent cutting underneath as the cutter swept over the grass. The next day, Jack went back over the grass with the conditioner. The spokes poked and separated the hay. Jack waited two days before he ran the baler over it. Square bales of hay dropped along the field behind him every few minutes until six o'clock that evening. By that night, Sheryl wouldn't let Abigail in the trailer. Abigail stayed with Jack in the trailer across the road. They sat in the floor. The couch had boxes of potpourri and naked baby dolls on it.

"You think this is the same bird?" Jack said. A baby bird was in his lap.

"Looks like it."

Jack nodded to himself. They cleaned Jack's trailer for a few hours. Abigail set the boxes that she thought Sheryl might want out on the front porch. In her digging through the back bedroom, she found a birdcage and brought it into the living room. She hung it on the hook near the back window and picked up the bird and set it inside.

"I don't think he likes it," Jack said. He opened the door and set the bird back down inside an empty cardboard box. Abigail set the birdcage out on the porch, along with some baby doll boxes. Henry was outside across the road, stepping down off the porch. Abigail kicked the birdcage and knocked a box of the naked baby dolls over. Legs and heads spilled down the steps. She ran across the road and into the yard. Henry ran around to the back of the trailer. Sheryl came out the back door and chased after him. When Abigail got to the path at the hayfield, Sheryl grabbed her by the shoulders.

"No Abby. You ain't seein' him like this. You hear me?" Sheryl said. Abigail watched her dad run down the path towards the fence. Sheryl turned Abigail around to face the back of the trailer and flung her hand towards it. "That's what you remember. Hold on to her, Jack." Jack walked behind and wrapped his arms around Abigail.

Next door, Abigail's mom stood on the top concrete step with her back door closed and looked out into the field behind Abigail. Birds called and sang. Sheryl came back a while later and walked up the wooden steps of her porch, rested the screen door against her heel for a moment, and went inside without shutting the big door behind her. The funeral was Sunday.

*

Everyone was out in the back yard. Sheryl fed the barrel hunks of wood and brush, and even threw in a few handfuls of hay throughout the night. Sheryl was talking to Henry's three brothers and one sister. They all had Budweiser cans in their hands. Abigail had only seen each of them a few times.

"That's just like Henry," the sister said. The preacher came over with a red can of Big K soda in his hand.

"Who told ya Henry liked Red Buttons, Mike?" Sheryl said.

"He'd always steal his comedy routines in the barracks. I don't think he ever knew we all knew they weren't his jokes," Mike said. Sheryl laughed.

Abigail's mom's back door swung open and Madeline came outside. Her porch light went off as she wandered over and crossed the property line. She wore a black dress and brown sandals. Her black and white hair was frizzed. The chatter in the backyard stopped. She walked over to Sheryl's back porch, stuck her hand in the cooler, and shook the water off a can of beer.

"I'm sorry for your loss," Madeline said. She pulled the tab on the can and chugged the beer. Sheryl tilted her head up to The Lord with her eyes closed and then dropped her head back down.

Abigail finished her fourth beer. She felt a swish inside her stomach as she dropped the can in the garbage bag under the porch. Madeline hugged her. Abigail returned the hug and walked down the path to the fence. She stood with her hands on it and watched Jack bend and stare over the piece of the barn door that was behind his easel. She went over the fence and shined her light at the paintings of little birdhouses on tall stands. Dark spots were blotted over the canvas.

Abigail became aware of her throat. It felt seasoned. "Uh-oh," she said with both hands on her stomach. She let the beer splash out of her mouth. It fell into her breasts and down her black dress. A wet strand of hair stuck to the front of her neck. She took a breath and felt something coming up again. Jack held her hair back the second time. He helped her up and steadied her before starting over the fence with her.

"Sorry I got it on your painting," Abigail said.

"It's okay." He walked her back down the path towards the trailer and let go of her when they got to the backyard. She waded through the cousins that were all men except for one their wives, past Pastor Mike who seemed to be the saddest one there, past her uncles who just kept nodding and laughing with Sheryl, past Karl who needed a pair of looser jeans, and past Madeline who was the only one who saw her go inside. She showered and brushed her teeth before she lay down in her bed. She rolled over into the dark emerald sheets that coiled up next to the wall.

Abigail couldn't fall asleep. Jack had the living room light on across the street. She lay there on her side and watched as Jack's torso would come up and go back down in the window. She got up and slipped into a pair of light brown sandals that she hadn't worn since she got back from Towson. She checked her hair with the camera in her phone and slipped out the front door.

She opened the screen door on the trailer across the road, letting it stay open against the wooden railing on the porch. She knocked on the big door just shy of the foggy window in the center. Jack opened it in his white t-shirt and red sweats. The bird chirped in his hand. He gently dropped the bird down inside the cardboard box in the floor in front of the couch. He walked back to the door with his hands in his pockets.

"Pick me up," Abigail said. Jack stood inside the doorway in his bare feet and scratched the scruff on his face. Abigail went towards him. He put his hands around her waist. He moved his head closer to hers. Abigail put her arms over his and he kissed her. They went into the trailer and Jack kicked the big door closed. Abigail closed the screen door when she left after the sun rose.

She crossed the road. There were still other cars and trucks out in front of her dad's yard. She looked up at the clouds that made the sky look like gravy as she walked up her dad's front porch. Across the property line, the lights in Madeline's trailer were off. The elephant ears sagged down over the side of her front porch.

Sheryl looked up from the kitchen table through her big squared glasses when Abigail went inside. Envelopes were scattered across the table and a pot of water boiled on the stove. Sheryl had the black binder out in front of her. It was open to one of the last few pages. Sheryl handed over a printed page. It listed faculty members of the Anthropology department at the University of Kentucky. Jack's black and white picture was there next to a name, Jay-Jackelson Austen. Sheryl scooted over a few of the envelopes on the table and Abigail opened one up and read it.

"They've been tryin' to buy the land ever since ya went to Towson," Sheryl said.

"But Jack just wants to paint the birds. That's what he said. He said he just wants to paint the birds." Sheryl slid over another letter, one signed by Henry and witnessed by Sheryl. It was her dad's will. "I don't understand. Why wouldn't he leave the farm to you?"

"This wasn't my farm, it was your daddy's. Now it's yours. You gotta make a decision, hon."

Abigail took the binder into her bedroom. Karl was asleep in her bed, so she closed the door and went into her dad's room. A body was asleep with their head turned away, facing the back wall of the trailer. Abigail sat herself down in an old recliner. The brown handle that brought up the footrest had been snapped in two ever since Abigail could remember. She opened the binder in her hands and examined the columns of mostly zeroes, nines, and ones. She read over one of the letters that had fallen in between the pages again. It was dated just a few months ago, February; the offer would probably still stand. Her distant uncle Lebanon got up out of bed and left the room. She read her dad's will again, then turned on and muted the morning news in the bedroom.

Abigail still hadn't figured much of anything out when it started getting dark outside. She saw a light on in Madeline's trailer through her dad's bedroom window. Abigail went out onto the back porch to watch her mom descend her concrete steps. She wore a thick black dress with sleeves that covered her arms. Madeline crossed the property line and walked along the path to the fence. Abigail followed her between the square hay bales. Madeline looked back at her as the back of her black dress glided along the dirt.

"It's alright, Abby," Madeline said. Madeline climbed over the fence and walked past Jack. He was painting a picture of a birdhouse from a model that he'd built with the wood from the barn door. It stood up on a two-by-four and was filled with bird seed. Madeline went further down into the grass, past the cockleburs and stopped after the dandelions, just before the purslane. Abigail ran over to her but the birds flew across her path. "There's nothing you can do," Madeline said. The birds glided around Madeline in a slow circle. She put out her arms and the birds flapped their wings and flew upward. "I can see Henry." She shouted and laughed as the birds flew faster around her. When the birds landed on their feet, Madeline fell. The funeral was Thursday.

There was a dinner around the kitchen table. Sheryl baked a roast in a plastic bag with potatoes and carrots. After dinner, Abigail went down the path. The birds were on the ground, walking along in the grass, pecking and pulling up worms and bugs and flapping their wings. Jack was painting a picture of a woman with birds on the ground around her. The woman in the picture had long black hair and wore a dark blue dress. She wore a green ring on her finger. The rifts in the dress made it hard to take her eyes away.

"Is this you?" Abigail said. Jack turned around and took the papers that Abigail was holding in her hand.

"I can explain."

"I think you should just go."

"Is that what you want?"

Abigail nodded. Jack went over the fence with his

paintbrush in his hand. Abigail moved the canvas on the top of the easel aside. There was another painting of a woman behind it. She looked a bit younger. The light source glazed her in a long blue and white shirt that stopped hanging just under halfway to the knees. She had fair skin and long black hair that rustled up away from her shoulders. Her legs and feet were naked and one foot was raised. Her arms were up over her head. Birds were flying around her.

Abigail could feel the birds around her lifting themselves up and flying past her, the rush of wind as she held out her arms and tilted back her head. She felt a hand pulling her back away from the wind. She whirled around and saw Sheryl. She held Abigail by the wrist. Abigail broke and started crying into Sheryl's shoulder.

They watched the birds fly around the easel. The birds landed and went back to pecking at the soil. Sheryl and Abigail climbed the fence, walked back up the path, past the hay bales, and went into the trailer.

Twenty-Dollar Bill

Trey made it up off his futon and onto his feet. He cleaned himself up and put a single slice of leftover pizza in the oven, a slice with more white cheese than yellow, and used a French press to brew ground coffee. He didn't have the energy to pump the milk to cream and he was out of sugar, so he drank it black. He took the brown bumpy mug over to the computer in front of the doorway and checked his email, not to check for anything new but to ponder what went wrong and dread just for a while longer the idea of moving back in with his mother. As he traced his financial decline through the archives of his email, he saw a twenty-dollar bill slide under the front door. There was a yellow note paper-clipped to it that read 209.

There was no one outside the door. He held the bill up to the cheap thirty-watt bulbs in the light fixture overhead, then took the money down to apartment 209 on his way to the grocery store for cleaning supplies. He buzzed the door and then knocked three times. After no one answered, he pushed the money under the bottom of the door and took the elevator down to the lobby and went to the store.

When he got back home, he checked the time on the top right of the computer screen. Moo was running away in his little plastic blue wheel, squeaking softly as he jogged. Trey had forgotten how much noise a hamster could make. He'd bought Moo with his last pain pill and five bucks for his son Ryan the first weekend that he was allowed an unsupervised visit with him. Ryan had wanted a pet, but Martha wouldn't allow pets in her house.

Trey rummaged through the boxes that had been stacked against the right wall in front of the kitchen and pulled out a bunny ear antenna. It took him a bit to find a good spot in the apartment for decent reception. He flipped through the channels. Some of them were working, some were pixelated, and then Trey couldn't remember exactly which station it was that Ryan liked to watch. He called his sister. She wasn't sure about it.

Trey cursed into the phone; Moo had bit his finger as he was feeding him.

His sister told him that hamsters stunk and that he knew he needed to get rid of it before he moved back in with Mom, right?

Trey spent the majority of the rest of the afternoon cleaning and throwing things that had accumulated in the corners of the walls into boxes. It was mostly old publications and articles that had to be tossed somewhere, but not out.

His door buzzed at around a quarter after seven. He made sure to fuss at Martha for being over an hour late. She didn't apologize; she stated that traffic in this area was terrible and that if Trey had gotten an apartment in a less congested area she'd be able to drop Ryan off in time.

She asked when he was going to tell her that he was moving. Trey hadn't given it much thought. He had to be out in two weeks; he was going to be out before then. Martha rolled her eyes. Ryan ran in between them into the apartment, straight to Moo, without saying a word. Trey invoked the paperwork and told her to get out of his apartment during his time with his son.

Ryan stared at Moo through the blue plastic cage. His right hand was stretched out over the side of it. Ryan's hand had grown wider and his fingers had grown a little longer over the past year. Ryan's other hand clutched onto a twenty-dollar bill and a yellow piece of paper that read 209.

Trey took the money and the paper from Ryan and left him in the company of Moo as he ran downstairs to apartment 209. He knocked. No one answered. He buzzed. He grasped and wiggled the doorknob, and the door opened. The apartment was empty and smelled like rubber. He went to the management office down in the lobby, but the office was closed for the weekend.

When Trey returned to his apartment, Ryan was still standing at Moo's cage. Trey asked Ryan if he was hungry, Buddy? Moo squeaked.

Trey had a half a box of cereal for them in the morning, and various colors of cans of whole potatoes and corn in his cabinet by the small stove. He paced for a few minutes, trying to remember what restaurant Ryan liked the best. He looked at the bill still curled up in his hand. He looked in the floor and traced his steps for the yellow paper. He opened the front door and poked his head into the hallway. He went back to the cabinet in his kitchen and opened the can of creamed corn and a can of potatoes.

Ryan had fallen asleep on the futon. Trey put the corn and potatoes in the refrigerator. He laid a brown towel down in the floor by the futon, carefully pulled one of the pillows out from under Ryan, and slept.

When Trey awoke the next morning, Ryan was standing at Moo's cage. Trey told him good morning. Ryan just stared through the plastic box, his hand planted firmly against its side as he watched the hamster sleep.

They ate cereal for breakfast, and then Ryan wanted to go outside and play. Trey walked him to a nearby park. Ryan got down on his knees and found an anthill. They watched the ants march through the grass with small pieces of a wrapper from a Milky Way bar, abandoned peanuts, something white, and various bits of other things that Trey couldn't recognize.

Trey took Ryan into the dollar store. He went right for the cheap toys. Ryan picked up a green box that said BUG KIT. It cost eighteen dollars. Trey gave the cashier the twenty in his pocket. For the rest of the afternoon, Ryan ran around the park with a net no bigger than his hand and occasionally came back to the bench with butterflies and alien bugs from hell. Trey opened the top of the little green cage. Ryan dropped the creatures down into the square opening. Trey helped Ryan pick up some dirt and grass and drop it down inside.

Moo was still asleep when they got back. He was lying with his head buried under the bedding of his cage. Ryan hit the cage walls over and over again until Trey had to pull him away from it.

Ryan asked Trey why his friend wouldn't wake up. Trey didn't know what to say.

Trey told him to get his things ready for when Mommy got there. After Martha took his son away, he went over to Moo's cage and lifted the lid. Trey let Moo rest in his palm as he walked slowly to the trash can.

One of the bugs in the green cage made a noise that sounded like running water. There was a knock at the door that night. A man in a gray t-shirt asked him if anyone had dropped off twenty bucks. Trey said no and closed the door.

You Haven't Seen Your Sister In A Year

You make it all the way to Lexington, Kentucky from College Park, Maryland, but you have to leave your black four-door Chevrolet truck parked outside Bee's and Betty's Diner to wait for your sister to drive down from Old School House Apartments to pick you up. She asks you how you've been. You say okay. She asks you if you'll go with her to her therapy session for group therapy night. You only agree to go because you're pretty sure Dad doesn't know she's even going to them.

White Christmas lights are draped over the tallest metal pole in the corner between Doc Park's Family Practice and H & R Block. Your sister parks the car in front of the only door that doesn't have any Christmas decorations already on it. You take your bag in with you. You follow your sister past the hand drawn turkeys with children's names and ages on them.

The therapist sitting in a lawn chair in the middle of the back of the room looks like a blond Jesus Christ with split ends. The largest family in the room is a mother, a father, a teenage boy, and a twenty-something girl. The twenty-something girl has the same posture as you do, slouched, your stomach curved in, comfortable, and completely unenthused. You watch the clock for the next thirty minutes while the father and son next to you discuss the son's addiction to eating pennies made before 1998. The bearded man on the other side of your sister has no one else with them. He hasn't spoken a word. The large family up front, which to be honest you still don't know the situation of, has spoken the most, even though the twenty-something girl hasn't even separated her lips since she sat down.

The Jesus therapist says Joely. You wait for him to continue. You say yes when he doesn't. He wants to know what you know about Anna's condition. He folds his hands and brings them up from his lap to the center of his chest. You wait to see if any doves fly up from behind him.

You say Anna is addicted to illegal cats. The Jesus therapist lowers his head and his eyes come closer to yours. He wants to know how you feel about your sister getting involved with illegal cats. You say that you just want to be able to visit for Thanksgiving without having to worry about illegal cats. The Jesus therapist wants to know the emotion. You say mad.

The Jesus therapist goes on, skipping any response from your sister and asking the man next to her if he wants to say anything. He shakes his beard and his toboggan no. The Jesus therapist turns back to the family of four. The twenty-something girl has her shoulders held up high and her ponytail is pressed against one of the snowflakes made from printer paper hung up on the sky-blue wallpaper. You could've sworn her hair was down before. Her foot shakes against the metal leg of the chair she sits in. She opens her mouth and puts both her hands over lips. The Jesus therapist says good job Debbie. He turns back to the father and son beside you. He asks the son about his penny-eating problem. The son says he has no pennies and turns out his pockets. The Jesus therapist says that's great, Zachary. The Jesus therapist says that it's so excellent that a lot of them are finding ways to deal on their own. You watch the choreography of his hands again as he claps them and moves them from the center of his chest back down to his lap. You laugh. The Jesus therapist asks you what.

You offer to make a deal. If your sister doesn't have a cat in her purse right now, you say that you'll pay for everyone's therapy session out of your own pocket. Your sister tells you not to be silly. You take your sister's purse, unzip the biggest zipper, and set the purse down in the middle of the room. You hear the contents of your sister's purse rustling before you even get back to your chair. A small orange and black spotted kitten purrs and pokes its wet nose that's too big for its head out at you. The cat's thin tail rises and waves at the Jesus therapist behind it. The kitten stares at the room through the crud in its eyes.

The Jesus therapist asks if it's a boy or a girl.

Anna says girl. You say your sister just wants her crazy check every month. The rest of the session was a waste of time.

Your sister takes too long to get back to the car after the therapy session is over. When your sister gets in the car, she leaves her purse unzipped. The kitten is gone.

Your sister drives away from the round street lamps around Main Street. Your sister says she's glad you came with her. She says she's dating someone. You turn your head towards her for the first time since she picked you up outside Bee's and Betty's Diner and say you're not meeting him. She says you're going to his house for Thanksgiving tomorrow. You hope you're able to drive back up to College Park tomorrow after your Dad arrives and fixes your car. You stare out the passenger side window until you see the white Old School House Apartments sign. Your sister gives you the keys to her apartment. You're still silently declaring that you're never going to ever meet your sister's boyfriend to yourself as you step out of the car and go into the last apartment around the curve at the back of the building.

A long-legged calico cat is outside playing with a red bologna string as you go inside. You're in the extra bedroom upstairs before you even hear your sister get the front door of the apartment closed behind her. There's no clock in the bedroom. Your work laptop with a REM sticker is unable to give you the time in anything except UTC-12. You don't know the password to your sister's wifi to check your work email so you lay the laptop next to you and lean your head against the slab of wood that seems to act as a visual replacement for the head of the bed.

You wake up with a sore neck. Just before you start down the light cream carpeted steps for orange juice that morning, there's a knock on the front door. You crack the door open. The Jesus therapist is standing outside. You cannot get over how much he looks like Jesus Christ, even in an unzipped black hoodie. He wears a blue shirt similar to the one he wore yesterday at the session. His blue jeans seem darker. He asks you if Anna is home. You hold the door as closed as you can without losing sight of him. Your body blocks the gap between the wall and the edge of the door. The cold wood of the door is against your ear. Your head is turned slightly to its side to appease the crick in your neck. You feel the brass of the doorknob slide along your palm, rolling out from under your pinky. The Jesus therapist sneakers up the stairs.

You go into the kitchen still thinking of orange juice. You open the fridge and scoot a few packages of bologna over with the side of a gallon of milk. You chug half a glass of milk on the way back upstairs. Your sister's bedroom door is shut. You stand for a minute listening for any meows on the other side of your sister's bedroom door. You hear the Jesus therapist laugh. You think that's how Jesus would laugh. You shake your head and go back inside the spare bedroom with your cold empty glass.

An orange and white cat rubs its face against your legs as you prepare a presentation for a proposed business site for when you go back to the office. You hear country music coming from your sister's bedroom. You wish that you had told Dad about your sister's cat problem every time you hear the Jesus therapist's voice across the wall. Your sister comes into the spare bedroom and says she's going next door to get the paperwork from the new tenants. You ask your sister about the cat. Your sister says that the cat is just Baby and he's not illegal.

You look the cat over. It's a bit too tall and the spots are a bit too round and plenty. It doesn't quite look like the ones you've read about, the mini tigers with Friskie's Special Blend in their whiskers or the black spotted mini panthers you caught your sister with the last time you were here.

You ask your sister for the wifi. She tells you it's in the notebook above the fridge. You lift your empty, milky glass up off the small brown nightstand between the bed and closet. The glass left a ring. You take it downstairs to fill it up with more milk. You lock the front door behind your sister.

You bump into the Jesus therapist on your way to the refrigerator. The Jesus therapist tells you that if you ever do anything that like that again, he will kill you. You don't think he's talking about you bumping into him. He takes a juice box from the fridge and sits in the chair nearest the air filter in the floor between the fridge and the table. You get the notebook from the top of the fridge. He lights a cigarette. You turn on the air filter and sit opposite him. You offer to pay him twenty-five thousand dollars to leave your sister. He puffs on his cigarette. You wait for the smoke to rise up from his ass. He says no thank you. You say thirty thousand. He laughs more playful than he did through your sister's bedroom door. He offers you a cigarette. You take one. You suck on it as he lights it for you. You cough. You hate menthols.

You hear Dad's black Chevrolet truck pull in and turn off in the visitor parking space nearest your sister's apartment. Dad unlocks the front door, puts a pie in the fridge, and sits on the couch. He says your truck is running fine. He offers to take you to Bee's and Betty's Diner. You say after you finish your cigarette. Dad introduces himself to the Jesus therapist. The Jesus therapist says he's heard so much about Dad and offers him a cigarette. Dad says no.

Dad asks you when you started smoking again when you get in his truck. You say a few minutes ago. Dad laughs and pulls out a pack of Marlboro Red 100s. You take one and roll down your window. You ask Dad if he knew how long Anna's been seeing the Jesus therapist. Dad says not long. Dad says he wishes you'd come by more often. You say you work a lot. Dad says he knows. You finish your cigarette before Dad pulls into the parking lot of Bee's and Betty's Diner. Your black truck is parked the furthest from the restaurant. Dad wants to drive your truck back to your sister's apartment, just to be safe.

Betty comes out of the restaurant. Betty asks you how you've been, kiddo. You say doing okay. Betty asks you what kind of work you're doing now. You say you manage real estate deals for a company that has contracts with retail businesses. Betty says like Cracker Barrel? You say like Target. Dad says thanks Betty. You drive Dad's truck and follow Dad back to your sister's apartment.

Dad's flip phone vibrates the dash. You answer it. A

guy wants to know about the apartment that's for sale. You say you mean for rent. The guys says no, for sale. You say Dad's not there right now and that he'll call the guy back soon. The guy says okay.

You park Dad's truck beside yours when you get back to your sister's. You brush off the cat hair from your back. You tell Dad someone called him about an apartment. He gets his flip phone out of his truck.

The Jesus therapist is helping a thin scruffy man in a navy blue suit load a metal toolbox from the storage under the apartments into the back of a red Ford. Your sister hands the scruffy man a package of bologna. The scruffy man hands your sister a large white envelope. The Jesus therapist waits until the scruffy man pulls out before he takes the envelope from your sister. Your sister announces it's time to go to the Jesus therapist's house. Your sister asks if they can all go in your truck, since it's bigger. The Jesus therapist asks you if you can haul another toolbox on the back. You say no. Your sister looks to Dad. Dad says all the toolboxes need to be out of storage soon. You say fine. Dad helps the Jesus therapist and your sister load three toolboxes onto the back of your truck.

Dad is in the passenger seat holding a pie on his lap. Your sister and the Jesus therapist are in the back holding Baby. The Jesus therapist's legs are poking into the back of your seat. A white car gets a little too close to you as you go through the light on Main Street. You speed up. Dad tells you to slow down. He holds the pie over his lap with both hands. The white car follows you all the way to the road that the Jesus therapist lives on in Lawrenceburg. It passes you when you pull into the driveway that the Jesus therapist says to turn in at.

There is a satellite dish against the front window of the red brick house. A short haired black and white cat is sitting outside the screen door. The garage is closed.

The kitchen is small. There is only one cabinet above the sink. The kitchen table is a cheap blue table with a soft surface and folded out legs. Your sister drops Baby into the kitchen floor. Baby goes under the table. The Jesus therapist takes the pie from Dad and puts it on the bottom shelf of the fridge. He pulls out a cold baked turkey and preheats the oven. You ask the Jesus therapist where the toolbox on the back of your truck goes. The Jesus therapist yells for Bobby.

The bearded man that sat next to your sister at the therapy session comes into the kitchen from living room. The Jesus therapist tells Bobby to get the toolbox off of your truck. Your sister tells you to help the Jesus therapist cut the potatoes. The Jesus therapist says no he's got it. You say you will help. Your sister goes outside with Bobby. The Jesus therapist offers Dad coffee. Dad says he just wants a glass of water. The Jesus therapist pulls out a cup from the cabinet and a pan from the bottom of the stove. The Jesus therapist pours dad a glass of water from a pitcher in the fridge and fills the pan with tap water while you peel and dice the potatoes. The Jesus therapist pours himself a mug of coffee and sits down at the table next to Dad.

The Jesus therapist tells Dad that your sister said that Dad had a master's degree in computer science from UK. Dad says that's right. Dad asks the Jesus therapist where he went to college. The Jesus therapist says two BS's and a MS in Psychology from UK. You ask to see the certificate. The Jesus therapist points to the fridge. The MS is hung up with a Burning Man magnet. The degree is dated May 2002.

Your sister comes back inside and whispers something to the Jesus therapist. You ask for salt and pepper. Your sister says it's in the cabinet. You open the cabinet up. Plates and cups are on one side. Cans and spices and boxes of macaroni and cheese are on the other. The Jesus therapist digs through the cabinet for you. He sets a box of macaroni and cheese down on the counter and hands you a large cylinder of Norton salt and a pepper grinder. You put too much salt in the potatoes after you pour them into the one nice blue bowl you find in the cabinet with a bunch of treble clefs blowing in gusts of wind all around it. You see black spots from the nonstick pan floating in the chunks of potatoes before you put the pepper in. The Jesus therapist starts a pan of macaroni and goes outside. You watch the water boil.

Dad asks your sister if anyone at Old School House Apartments was late on their rent this month. Your sister says no. Dad says to remind him to get the receipt book before he leaves. Your sister says she will. You blend and whip the mashed potatoes in the white Kitchen Aid in the corner.

The Jesus therapist comes back inside with Bobby and pulls out a square plastic bowl with a lid over it. He puts it in the microwave for three minutes. You present your mashed potatoes in the nice blue bowl. Dad pulls out the pie he made from the fridge and sets it on the corner of the table. Your sister pulls out a brown glass baking dish of pasta salad from the middle shelf of the fridge and sets it on the table near her seat. The Jesus therapist pulls the turkey out of the oven and slices it with an electric knife.

A black cat rubs its face against your red chinos.

The macaroni boils over. The Jesus therapist drains the water from the macaroni. Bobby fills everyone's glasses with iced tea from the fridge. Your sister takes three slices of bologna from the hoard of it in the crisper in the bottom of the fridge and pulls off the red strings. She slings the bologna and the strings out the screen door in different directions. Your sister gets out two more pieces of bologna and drops one down for the black cat and one down for Baby. Dad takes the first bite of turkey. You wait until last.

Dad asks the Jesus therapist how the therapy business is. The Jesus therapist says pretty alright. You ask how much he makes. Your sister calls you rude. You say you could just Google it anyway. The Jesus therapist says about one hundred thousand a year. Dad brings up that he got a computer science degree and that it didn't do him any good in the real estate business. The Jesus therapist laughs. Dad laughs with him. Your sister laughs. Bobby smiles and dips his turkey in his mashed potatoes.

Baby hisses at the other cat for trying to take his bologna string. Your sister says Baby. The Jesus therapist says Bandit.

You ask where the bathroom is. The Jesus therapist says at the end of the hall. The black cat follows you to the bathroom. You block the cat from entering with your foot and close the door. You sit on the toilet seat with your head in your hands. Something in the kitchen falls. Your sister screams Baby really loud. You wait for the cat fighting from the kitchen to stop before you flush, wash your hands, dry them on a towel covered in cat hair, and go back down the hall.

There is a knock at the screen door. Your sister answers it. It's dark outside. Your sister turns on the porch light. A scruffy man in a suit is outside the door.

Your sister goes outside with him. You walk up to the door to shut it. Bobby pushes you outside.

A bright white light disrupt your peripheral vision on your right side and you stumble with your palms out in front of your face down the gravel driveway until you hit your truck with your hands. The toolbox is still on the back of your truck. The lock has been cut open. The bright white light atop an unmarked white car is in your face, shining towards the Jesus therapist's house. Two uniformed officers from the outskirts of the glow around you step into the light and point their guns up at you. One of them is saying slowly, slowly. You hear your sister crying from the back of a nearby police car. You say Dad's still inside as the officers cuff you and walk you to a second police car. A group of officers pry the garage open with a long metal rod. There are large orange and black spotted cats inside, one of them licking their paws, the other pacing. The pair of officers that cuffed you enter the Jesus therapist's house and bring out Dad with his hands behind his back. Bobby brings the Jesus therapist out and walks him by the cuffs around you and on out of the light before you. An officer reads you your rights. You look at your sister through the car window. You say that when you get out of this you won't ever come back.

Wine And Dine

He was standing there hunched up outside the doorway of the black-bricked restaurant across the street. His body was turned away from me, away from the wind. Smoke rose up in between his face and the building as I walked closer to the bus stop at 5th and Broadway. His hair was shorter than it had been. I stopped myself from trying to figure out if I liked the back of his head or not when I got to the lamppost with the bus sign on it, my shadow interrupting the yellow glow from the streetlamp that had caked the snow on the sidewalk. I shivered.

"You got the time?" He shouted at me from across the street. I forgot what time meant. I waved and he asked again.

"Twenty-six after nine," I said. He wobbled his head, waved, and then turned back around. I watched him put his cigarette out against the black brick and toss it in the bin near the trashcan, his right hand in his dark stained blue jeans pocket the whole time. The bus pulled up and I went home.

The next Monday night, the bus stop sign had moved over to the other side of 5th street, bolted to the lamppost in front of the restaurant. He was there again like he always was at a quarter after nine.

"Seen you around," he said. Tonight he was wearing black fitted jeans and a white hoodie. The string from the hood only hung down the right side of his neck. His hair was brown, darker than mine. He was clean-shaven. I couldn't tell what color his eyes were. I had to say something back, anything, but he held out a red and white cigarette box. I took a cigarette and started coughing before he even finished lighting it. He laughed. "I'm John."

"Nick." I stood there, letting the heat from the cigarette move closer to my fingers. I shivered as the wind blew through the back of my thin jacket. I could see the places on his face where his skin had started to stretch around his cheeks, under his eyes. I could see now that they were brown. He looked to be in his early thirties.

I saw a red and blue bus at the light a few blocks down. I walked over to the black brick and scratched the cigarette across the exterior of the restaurant. When the bus stopped, I climbed up. The machine swallowed my two dollars and I sat down in a seat near the back, my khaki bag in the seat beside me. I could see him through the windows as I rode away. His hand tugged on the string that hung from his neck.

Tuesday, the bus stop was back on the other side of 5th street, opposite the restaurant. A little black kid stared me down as he passed me while I waited near the sign. A man held onto his wrist. When they started across the sidewalk, the kid kicked himself up off of the ground, nearly pulling the man down over top of him. The man cursed the kid and pulled him across the street. The kid tried the maneuver again, knocking over a menu that was written on a dry erase board. They disappeared down Broadway.

He came out of the restaurant across 5th street.

I watched him bend over and pick up the board of multi-colored scribbles, checking its alignment and scooting it over a few inches. He was wearing black jeans and a black t-shirt with white letters all over it that was half tucked under his belt. His belly was pooched out. His eyes caught me on their way down towards his hands, his fingers already pulling something out of his pocket. The light from the neon open sign hit his face just right and his top was twisted just enough to make it look like he had abs over his stomach.

He turned his head over towards me. I looked away and forced my eyes to stay toward the wig store across

Broadway. It was called Wig Haven. I could see two mannequin heads in the display window, one wearing a dark short wig and another with a long blonde wig. I examined their faces and tried to see if the short haired one had makeup on, but I only saw the dark white face, identical in almost every way to the one beside it.

I checked the time with my phone and let some air seep out of my nose, making it the tallest part of my body for a stretch. That's when I noticed that the sign I was under was actually a NO PARKING sign. The bus passed me up as I was crossing 5th street, when I blew out what little air I had left in me. My breathing sped up and nothing I thought of made it stop. I spun around, clenching my ribs. He caught me as I was falling over. He walked me inside the restaurant and sat me down at a dark green booth, as dark as the leaves of the skinny trees planted in front of every few lines of the sidewalk outside.

"You alright?" He asked. There were orange crumbs in the corner of the charcoal gray table near where my left arm had landed. The salt shaker to the right looked out of place, too far from the pepper, and one of the napkins had almost fallen out of the holder, one of the edges of it still stuck to the napkins behind it. The restaurant was quiet. There were two young men at the table to my left and a teenager who was eating with a woman who looked to be about thirty at a booth behind me.

"I missed my bus," I said.

"Water," he said. He looked to one of the male waiters. They brought me a glass with no ice. They poured water in it right in front of me from a pitcher that I could see water spots on. I rested my head back against the soft back of the booth. I stared at the wall beside the window as he walked away, the dark green paint bouncing back at me. The gray trims around the window matched the tabletops. One of the other waiters brought me a basket of wheat bread. I broke off a half and ate it. I didn't see John until after the woman and the teenager behind me had left and the couple beside me had asked for their check. He came out of the back, his hands smothered in white powder. "You okay now?"

"Fine." I put the pinch of bread I'd been caught with back in the basket. He handed me my bag by the strap.

"You left it outside."

"Thank you." I unfastened the plastic clip and skimmed the contents. I pulled out a stick of gum from the bag after I was sure I'd found everything I brought with me, my black and white checkered notebook with sewn pages, my red ink pen that wrote black, a new reprint of The Adventures of Huckleberry Finn in between a manila folder and my friend Malaysia's first book that she'd given me a copy of at work earlier that day.

"We close in about thirty minutes. You need a ride?"

The two men at the table beside me kissed.

"I'm fine. Thank you so much." I pulled out a wad of cash from my wallet and John waved his hands.

"No, no."

The couple scooted their chairs out and stood up. The one with the glasses went towards the bathroom and the taller one with the tan pulled his wallet out from his back pocket and dropped some cash on the table. John thanked them for coming. The man who brought the bread walked over and collected the tip. I texted Malaysia. The man with the glasses held the door open for me.

"You sure you don't need a ride?" John stretched his arms.

"Are you sure you don't mind?" I let the door close.

He shook his head and I slipped my phone back into my left pocket. He did some stuff at the register while the rest of the staff cleaned, then he led me to his yellow Kia that was parked at the end of the block.

"Which way?" He asked after he got in an unlocked the passenger side door.

"That way, towards Cecil. Ten minutes."

"Ten minutes? That's not bad." He started the car and carefully pulled out into the street. The streetlamp shut off and I watched the black bricks of the restaurant fade into the dark. He rolled down his window, picked up a green lighter, and lit a cigarette. He stuck the Marlboro box out towards me. I waved it away. He set the box down inside a rectangular opening where it looked like the radio should have been. I could hear his nose pinching the air in between his puffs. His brown eyes looked over at mine. He let me look into them longer than he should have, driving. His eyes were so big that it felt like he would have let me stay in there with him forever.

He drove west and kept quiet. There was hardly any traffic until a dark green Chevy Blazer passed. I could see the face that the woman made as I sat there. Her eyes, nose, and mouth were all squished together as she rolled past. She didn't take her eyes off of me until she had to at the light ahead. That's when I first remember thinking that I wasn't a man.

"Cecil's up here," I said, but he had already started to slow down.

"Gotcha." He tossed his cigarette butt out and rolled up the window before turning left. He turned his head towards me.

"Keep going. Up there." He drove past the gray stone church that marked the block that my apartment building was on. "Right here." He stopped the car. "Thanks for the ride."

"Anytime." I stepped out with my bag and shut the door. "You have to slam it." He coughed as I opened it and closed it again, and then I waved at the car as he drove away.

I never had to ask John for a ride again. My friend Malaysia, from my office at the university, started taking me home. Wig Haven closed a few years ago. I have one of the mannequin heads from the window display in my bedroom on my dresser. They gave it to me when I bought my longer brown hair from there before it closed. I practiced putting makeup on it for months before I'd even try to put it on my face.

Malaysia came with me my first night out as a real woman, when my hair had grown out and my breasts were real. She did my makeup for me, a light blush and base, nothing too over the top. She wanted me to wear a flowing white dress with a brown lace that made me look like I was going on a date with seven dwarves. Her fashion choices were questionable, even to someone like me who didn't know their way around a Cato's yet. She was born into a large family from Bulgaria. She had gorgeous long blonde hair and she wore a short faded turquoise dress.

She wanted to know where I wanted to eat. John's restaurant was the first place I'd thought of. I hadn't been back to it in years. I didn't even know the name.

The restaurant was busy. We had to wait thirty minutes for a table to clear. The tables were clean and bare. The room was much brighter than I remembered. The booths around the walls were now a light wooden brown. The tables were white with thin beige chairs. The number of tables had been reduced. On this side of the wide pillar in the middle of the room was a black statue of a horse. Its leg muscles were gleaming under the light; the hair in the mane and tail were frayed all the way to their ends and there were ruffles in the fur down towards the bottom near the legs that went under the belly. I caught Malaysia staring at me like she had been staring for a few months.

"This is a beautiful place," she said as a baby-faced guy in a white dress-shirt and black pants handed us our menus. "Cameron Red's Diner. I don't think I've ever had red wine." She looked over her menu.

"You should try the Merlot," I said.

She agreed and I had the same. Our waiter brought us some water and poured Malaysia and I each a glass of wine from a fat necked bottle. I remembered the guy who brought the bread out to us a few minutes later.

"They have salmon," Malaysia said. I finally turned my menu to the entrées. They didn't have much to choose from: a roast duck, a glazed salmon, a lemon chicken. The sides were a choice between a pile of lettuce with some some tomatoes and a pickled onion or a soup that changed daily. I silently settled on ordering the duck as my main course. As Malaysia continued to look down at the menu, I tried the bread and looked around for John.

"Are you lovely ladies ready to order?" The waiter said.

"I'll have the duck," I said.

"Nice choice. And for the side? We have a potato soup today."

"The salad."

"For you, ma'am?"

"What are the seasonings on the salmon?"

"There's a little paprika, some parsley, a little pepper, no salt I know. The bourbon glaze over it is really sweet." Malaysia turned her nose up to the word "paprika".

"Can I get that without the paprika?"

"Oh, but that's what makes it good!" Malaysia shook her head. The waiter nodded and scribbled on his notepad. "Will you be having dessert?"

"No," we said.

"Alright, I'll take the menus out of your way." The waiter smiled and walked away.

"Did you see the horse?" I pointed behind Malaysia towards the white pillar. She turned and humored me with a smile.

"I don't understand why everyone is so horse crazy here."

"Derby is coming in a few months. Ever been?"

"I went when I first moved here, years ago. I couldn't handle the smell." Malaysia tried the bread. She chewed on it with a confused face.

"The bread was better the last time I was here. I think the place had a different name. Not sure what is was. It changed a lot." I continued to look for John. I peeked behind me to see if he was standing outside smoking. The waiter came back to check on our drinks. "Did this place used to have a different name?" I asked the waiter.

"I'm not sure," he said.

"Can you please find out?" The waiter smiled after my request and walked to the red wooden podium that was near the doors to the kitchen. He tapped the shoulder of a large woman with a squashed face. She shook her head and went through the doors. The guy who brought the bread emerged from behind the doors and the waiter pointed at our table. The guy who brought the bread walked over to us.

"Hi. I'm Walden. Did you have a question about the restaurant?"

"I was just wondering if you knew what it was called a few years ago?"

"Before the new owner bought it, it was called John Smith's Wine and Dine."

"Is John still around?"

"No, he moved to Florida. I think he passed away a few years ago. He had cancer." Walden left.

"Was he a friend?" Malaysia asked.

"I knew him."

"I'm sorry." She sipped her wine. I reached for mine and found it empty.

"Do you like the wine?"

She had barely started on it.

"It's alright." She blinked a few times. Our food came out and she scooted her glass an inch away from her. I pulled my cup closer to me and asked for more wine. He was back with a glass before I finished my first bite of meat. I took a gulp and set my glass back down. Malaysia pointed at me when I looked up. Her top lip was raised and her teeth were showing. I followed her finger to my left breast. There was a drop of wine on the white dress she had me wearing.

"Oh shit, I'm sorry." I didn't know what to do about wine stains and from the look on her face, Malaysia didn't know either.

"The lace kind of covers it." She smiled. I stuffed a little of the lace into my cleavage and let it hang over the stain. I took another drink and another bite of the duck. It tasted medium well. I put my fork down. Malaysia picked at her salmon.

"Thank you for coming out with me tonight," I said.

"Happy to do it. You look so beautiful."

I smiled at her before reaching for my wine glass again. Malaysia scratched her fork against her plate, flaking the salmon apart. After the last gulp of my wine, I pushed myself up with my legs. I heard the white dress rip beneath me. Malaysia continued to separate the meat of her salmon from the skin, sliding it over into the corner with her fork. The waiter was at the table next to me. He turned his head. I turned my head sharply at him. The older couple that was eating at the nearby table stopped chewing. With my eyes, I begged the waiter to not say anything as I walked to the restroom.

In the mirror, I noticed the brown goo from the duck sauce stuck to the lace. I hovered my hands under the paper towel dispenser and wet the brown paper in the sink. I tried to rub the goo off with the paper in between my thumb and index finger, but it just turned the lace into a damp black mess. My eyes felt heavy.

There was a knock on the door.

"You alright?" Malaysia said. I opened the door a crack and peaked out.

"Can you take me home?"

"What's wrong?"

"I just want to go home."

"Alright. Come on."

"No. Just go get the car and I'll come outside." Malaysia stared for a moment and then walked back to the table. I watched her through the crack of the door, both my hands clutching the long gold handle, my thumb pressing on the lock. Malaysia spoke to the waiter and he brought her the check. She gave him her card and put a green bill down on the table. She looked back at the restroom before she grabbed her purse and went outside. A minute later, I ran past the black horse, tapping my hand on its back as I hurried past. I stepped out the door and looked for Malaysia's silver car. It was dark. I forgot that Malaysia had to park a few blocks down. I could see the car coming down from the right. I felt a breeze down my back as I ran towards her. She stopped the car and I climbed into the passenger side. I felt my purse in the floorboard under my feet. I still forget it sometimes.

"What's going on? Are you okay?"

"I'm fine." I wiped my eyes.

She turned the car around and drove towards Cecil. When she got to the stone church, I picked up my purse and thanked Malaysia for the ride home. She stopped the car outside my apartment building and stared at me in her seat. "Want to go to Florida over spring break?" She said. The thought occurred to me that maybe I would find John alive and well, maybe running a nice restaurant near one of the beaches. I thought about the shape of his head overtop a tie-dye shirt and swimming trunks.

"I'll think about it."

Malaysia moved her head slowly over the armrest. I fiddled around in my purse for my key fob. It had fallen into my copy of The Adventures of Huckleberry Finn in my purse and had crinkled the middle ten pages or so. I dropped my purse when her lips touched mine. A few minutes later I adjusted the pages and mashed the cover flat. I opened the passenger side door and darted towards my apartment when the light in the car came on. I don't even remember if I shut the car door for her. I unlocked the lobby doors and took the stairs up to my apartment. I tossed my keys on the dresser next to the mannequin with brown hair and took off the ruined dress, but then I had the best night's sleep I'd ever had as Nikki. It was probably the wine.

The Audience

Instead of spending his busboy check on the new bed, Cody spends it on an upgrade for his blog. He writes about the best chocolate chip cookie in Louisville with a smile that afternoon and finishes the workday with a sigh. He washes all the laundry. He doesn't fold Jared's.

He dusts the living room before Jared gets home. He would've left for a burger alone if he'd have watched the time better. He brushes off the coffee table as Jared's keys scratch through the lock.

Jared lets out a groan as his keys are removed with a step backward then two forward. He kicks off his shoes against the tall black floor lamp and drops a new shirt hanging from a plastic hanger onto the nearest arm of the couch.

Cody tickles the bookshelf where a clutter of graphic novels, trade paperbacks, and cookbooks stand against themselves, squished between two brown maple shelves. A paperback laughs as the yellow feathers slide against the sky blue spine.

"Cook anything?" Jared peels his socks from around his ankles.

"I pulled some of the hamburger out yesterday. Spaghetti?" Cody shakes the duster at the books.

Jared slides his lower lip to the left. He tosses his socks onto the couch. "Kinda feeling like Chinese."

"If you want. How was work?" Cody dusts the top of the shelf. Jared is too close, stripped to his white t-shirt and red shorts.

Cody runs the duster vertically down the spines. He holds his breath and puffs his lips. A book with a deep voice giggles. Cody breathes. He lightly taps them, one by one.

"New girl. Doesn't know anything about tolling. Did you have a good day off?" Jared asks.

The giggler, a large glossy red book, giggles again as he lightly taps the duster against it. "I was busy with the blog," Cody says.

"Who had the best toast in town this week?" Jared grips Cody's hips. His hands tighten after Cody faces him. The books hush their own whispers behind them.

"Best chocolate chip cookie." Cody pushes away and steps toward the fake marble table in front of the kitchen. "There's room in your closet now." Jared's hands fall to his own thighs. The audience sighs.

Jared picks up his new shirt by the hook. He walks his new button-up and dirty socks down the hall.

Cody places the duster on the end of the table. He browns the hamburger.

An hour later, the books cough as smells of tomato sauce and teriyaki waft into the living room from the kitchen.

Losing One

The rain stopped hitting the tin roof above the garage door. Sean turned off the table saw and wiped the sawdust from his face with his faded red t-shirt. Maggie ran out from under the silver Nissan. She shook the water off her and sat down on her hind legs. She scratched behind her ears and breathed through her mouth. Sean put his arms out and she ran to him. She hung off his shoulders and licked the wood pieces off his face.

"Easy now, Maggie. How long have you been over here? They're prolly looking for you." The smell of rain and watered-down sweat choked him. He stood up and patted out his jeans and t-shirt. Maggie leaped off her front legs and dropped back down as she turned. Sean flipped the switch on the inside of the garage and ducked under as the door came down. He walked down his driveway, across his yard, past the water meter and lighting rod, toward a red and brown brick house. Sean stepped from his overgrown yard into the well-clipped lawn of his next-door neighbors'. He scratched his throat with a cough at the smell of herbs and ground bark. Maggie wagged her tail through an overgrown tomato garden between his house and theirs. He went around it and past the pea green Charger in the driveway.

Maggie ran through the grass toward the side door of the brick house. Sean followed the flat round stones. The screen door opened before either of them reached the house.

"Oh my God. I don't know how she always manages to get out when it rains," Stacey said. The dog ran in through the open screen door. "Maggie, stay there, no, there." She yelled and pointed into the kitchen on the right. Maggie's tail fell onto the linoleum, then she stood and ran onto the carpet in the living room. Stacey threw her hand up and shook her head.

Stacey was a woman in her mid-thirties with black shoulder-length hair. Sean would never admit to her or her husband, Frank, that he could see some gray on her head as she leaned out the door and into the sun as light glided across the yard.

"How are you, sugar?" Stacey grabbed her purse by the stand under the light switch and stepped outside.

"Oh, you know, getting a little done with this and a

little done with that." He rubbed the back of his head and smiled.

"Uh-huh, aren't we all? Casey here yet? Figured you two'd already have your guns out." She scratched her ear then felt inside her purse. Her long earrings flashed in the beams of sun. Sean looked away.

"Not yet. A few hours, probably. You know Miranda." Sean popped his knuckles.

"Uh-huh. Frank's in the basement. Careful, he's got that mess with the tomatoes down there." Stacey pulled her keys from her purse. When the Charger backed out of the driveway, Sean went inside. He took off his shoes as the screen door shut. Maggie put her front paws onto Sean's shirt. She ran them down his jeans and lifted them to the shirt again. Sean rubbed her head. She dropped down onto the carpet. Sean took a step into the living room. Maggie followed. He lifted her up with both hands under her belly and carried her to the open basement door. She ran down the blue steps. Sean followed her down.

The basement smelled like a stewed garden. White boxes were tossed behind the pillar ahead of the steps. More boxes and totes were stacked along the left, stopping just before the refrigerator. The yellow fridge door was left open. Sean pushed it shut, careful not to touch the brown stains on the door.

Maggie sat down by Frank at the stainless-steel pot

of tomatoes on the deep freezer in the corner. She wagged her tail. Frank's white and red Louisville shirt was clean until he grabbed a gob of tomato and dropped it onto her face. She pulled the pulp in with her tongue before it fell over and off her snout. Juice dripped onto the concrete.

"Casey here yet?" Frank said.

"Not yet." Frank turned his head away from the glass jars and funnels.

"That's not like Miranda is it? You call them?" Frank picked up the basket of sugar and sifted through it with a little yellow spoon.

"Casey's a teenager now. Probably busy with boys." Sean put on the oven mitt lying on the freezer door.

"Uh-huh. Or Miranda is." Frank dropped a small amount of sugar inside each funnel.

"We're going hunting when she gets here. You can come with us if you want," Sean said. He leaned into the freezer and smiled. A jar fell into the floor. He knelt beside the shattered pieces.

"Use the broom. You'll cut yourself." Frank closed the sugar. Sean tossed the glass into a plastic trash can under the back of the stairs with his hands and put back on his oven mitt.

Frank grabbed the handle of the pot in front of him with a towel. Sean grabbed the other handle. They walked the big pot over the jars along the freezer together and let the tomatoes fall into the funnels.

"You were gonna do this by yourself without a ladle?" Sean asked. He stumbled into Frank's ribs. He let his elbow rest under Frank's armpits.

"I would've managed." Frank held the pot still over the last jar in the first row. It was full. "Ready?" Frank waited. Sean let Frank's weight hold him a moment more.

"Ready." They leaned forward and took the pot the other way across the freezer. They sat the pot back down when the last jar was filled. Maggie jumped up and rubbed her paws on Frank's Louisville shirt as he walked with the pot towards the staircase.

"Down Maggie," Frank said. Maggie tried her luck with Sean. He held up his hands, palms out. Maggie whined. Sean reached out and scratched behind her ears. She jumped up onto him and ran her paws down his shirt.

"Maggie, come on," Sean said.

"Down Maggie," Frank said from upstairs. Maggie went to the far side of the basement, between an old dresser and more boxes. She laid down beside the dresser and spread all four of her legs across the concrete.

Frank came downstairs with a clinging pan. The steam from it had fogged his glasses. He sat the pan on the freezer, removed his glasses, and wiped his face with his long sleeve.

"What'd you end up getting Casey for her birthday?" Frank grabbed the tongs from the steaming pan and placed a lid on a jar.

"Some game she wanted." Sean squeezed a cut on his ring finger.

"She plays video games?" Frank placed another lid.

"No, a board game. Some kind of talking game with a mouthpiece that makes it hard to talk." Sean went to the sink by the refrigerator. He pulled the lever up and watched the blood spill down the drain.

"That sounds like Casey." Frank tightened a ring around a lid. "You alright? Looks like you're canning your own set of tomatoes over there."

"Should've used the broom." Sean held his finger under the running water and then applied pressure.

Frank went to the shelf above the top of the steps and returned with a small bandage. Sean wrinkled a paper towel from the holder on the side of the fridge into his hands, then he finished by wiping them onto his red shirt. He reached for the bandage.

"Let me." Frank peeled the paper off and removed the tabs. Sean pointed his finger below Frank's chest. Frank lifted Sean's hand up to his eyes, then he pulled the hand back down by the wrist and rolled the bandage up over the finger. He lifted his glasses from his nose and sat them up higher as Sean wiggled his digits at him.

Frank stared past Sean's fingers. He leaned Sean back onto the edge of the sink. Sean held onto Frank's arms.

"Stacey?" Frank asked. His hands were around Sean's lower back.

"She left." Sean lifted his thighs away from the sink. Frank held him tight. Their lips mashed and their jeans unzipped. When they got off, they cleaned themselves up with paper towels and water from the sink. Frank cleaned his glasses with his shirt and went back to the freezer. He grabbed the tongs, pulled a lid out of the water, and set it on top of the next jar.

Sean fixed his brown hair and felt of his pockets.

"Where's my phone?" Sean looked around the sink and through the steps to the freezer.

"You didn't have it out none," Frank tightened a ring around a lid. The jar busted. Glass shattered over the concrete. "Shit. Lose one every time." He slid in his socks across the floor and stopped between the two shelves in the corner along the sink wall. He pulled a broom from behind the furthest shelf and grabbed some paper towels from the holder by the fridge. Maggie wagged her tail on the other side of the steps. She jumped up onto Frank as he came back over to the red splattered glass. "Down, Maggie, down." She whined and came over to Sean.

"No, Maggie," Sean said. She jumped up onto him and ran her paws down his shirt. He grabbed them and held onto them. They danced while Frank swept and wiped up tomatoes. Frank held his palms out to Sean after he finished.

"No cuts," Frank wiped the excess tomato juice from his hands onto his shirt. He pulled another lid up from the water with his tongs and set it on a jar. Sean set Maggie's paws down as she licked his wrapped finger. He pulled his hand up and Maggie turned around. The side of her blonde coat was red.

"Hey Frank, Maggie's bleeding."

"What?" Frank dropped the tongs into the pot and squatted by Maggie. He examined her coat. Sean went to the sink and pulled the roll of paper towels off the holder. He got down next to Frank, who looked at him from over the top of his glasses.

"It's tomato," Frank said. Maggie licked his glasses. He cleaned them with his shirt and went back to the jars. Sean ran a paper towel over Maggie's side. She darted away. He tossed the towel into the trash under the stairs and put his hands in his pockets. He looked around the basement from under the stairs.

"You sure I didn't have my phone down here?"

"You wanna use our phone to call?" Frank pointed upstairs.

"No. I'd better get I guess. You wanna come hunting with us later?" Sean watched Frank tighten the lid around the jar.

"Come back later."

"Okay." Sean went up the stairs and walked through the house. He put on his shoes and went out the door.

The sun hid behind the clouds. Sean walked along the grass-grown stones, across the empty driveway, past the garden, over the lawn, and through his overgrown yard past the lightning rod. It started to rain before he got past the water meter. He went through his front door and into the garage. His phone was on his saw table. He slid his bound finger across the screen. It took a few tries. No missed calls. He called Casey. No answer. He opened the garage door and watched it rain.

His phone vibrated in his hand. It was an unknown number. He slid his unbound finger across the screen.

"Hello?" Sean dropped the phone. He picked it back up.

"Hey, Dad," Casey said. Her voice was low and raspy.

"Casey? Where are you two?"

"Mom's in the hospital." Sean put his hand over his hip.

"What happened?"

"She wasn't feeling good this morning and she came in and they're keeping her." Rain pounded the tin roof of the garage.

"Do you want me to come get you?" Sean listened to Casey's breath.

"No. I'm gonna stay here."

"Okay."

"Okay. Love you, Dad."

"Love you."

Sean put his phone in his pocket. Maggie ran across his driveway and under the Nissan, wearing her tomato stains. He turned on his table saw and split a two-by-four.

An Interpretation

Works Cited
Frost, Robert. "Mowing."

He let the phone ring until he got his voicemail and almost left him a loud one, but he swiped the phone call away after only leaving a breath or two. His partner hadn't showed up to meet with the first two clients and Richard was almost late to meet his 11 o'clock himself. Richard was contemplating trying Craigslist. He tried one more time to reach Jake as he slipped into his thin blue button up. There was no answer. He put his cell in his pocket and then tucked his shirttail into the khakis before leaving through the front door.

He followed the sidewalk down two blocks, watching the orange arrows and red circles painted along it. He never could quite memorize their patterns or their order. He was always seeing them for the first time. The only one he didn't seem to be able to ever forget was the one on the other side of the stoplight. It had tilted red lines with two ones or tally marks, or lines, he was never sure, painted under them. The two sides of the carrot that pointed straight ahead were slightly darker than the two tally marks, as if they had been painted after the tally marks themselves.

He arrived at the last red circle just before Mrs. Calli's. He stopped for a few seconds when he saw Mrs. Calli standing on her porch. She was standing too far from the door to be using it or the house itself for any support, and there weren't any beams along the edges of the porch for her. She peered out over her yard, her long gray hair hanging dead and stiff from her head.

"Richard, is that you?" Mrs. Calli said. He didn't bother responding. She wouldn't be able to hear him. "Is it? You're slow. You're alone? Where's your young one. I've got a letter that needs to go out today. Got to get to the post office. Don't let me forget."

"Good morning, Mrs. Calli. I'll take your letter as I go, Mrs. Calli." Mrs. Calli held out her elbow with her hand on her hip suspiciously high. She held onto the envelope with her other hand, crumpling the paper and the return address in the corner. "It'll need a stamp," Richard said. He grasped the free end of the envelope. She didn't let go.

"Ain't got none. Weren't you listening? You deaf? I gotta go to the post office."

"Alright, Mrs. Calli." Mrs. Calli released her grip. Richard dropped his hand down to his side, letting the envelope rest against his navy-blue pants. Mrs. Calli opened her screen door and turned her head towards Richard before slowing down as she went through, grabbing onto the doorframe as she stepped on inside. The screen door squeaked. Richard waited for her to clear the way before he stepped inside himself. A strong funk hit his nose. Mrs. Calli pulled herself slowly into the kitchen. First, she hauled herself around with one hand on the island. Then, with a glance back at Richard, two.

The kitchen had been used today. A stove covered of salt sprinkles sat in the corner on the opposite side of the busy counter from the refrigerator, which was left open. A cup of coffee was on the table. The coffee pot was still on, jammed between a crockpot and a Foreman grill, nearly empty. A thick hardcover book was on the table in the center of the room, though the jacket had been removed. The lid on the trashcan against the wall in the back, adjacent to the stove, was propped open with microwaveable meal boxes. The top box still had food inside it.

Mrs. Calli made it to the sink and bent down so low that Richard couldn't see her behind the island again until she came back up with a blue bottle of Dawn. She turned on the water.

"Been cleaning all morning." She raised her chin and rubbed her eyes, turned around, and went to her coffee cup.

Richard turned away from the kitchen and walked past the sofa, around the coffee table with stacks of newspapers, romance novels, and the back cover of the television remote on it. He stopped at a tall chest of two drawers at the back of her living room. On top of the drawers were cardboard boxes, the top of which Richard knew was full of patterns. In front of the boxes was a small weekly medication box with letters for each weekday printed on top. The "W" compartment was already empty. He turned to see if Mrs. Calli was looking in his direction. She wasn't; she had her face buried in the book on the kitchen table. The water was still running.

He placed the envelope in his hand down on the edge of the dresser and lifted the lid off the top box of patterns, raising his right arm over his head. He felt as far down and around into the box as his arm would let him. He felt nothing but patterns. He took his arm out. After a quick check to see if Mrs. Calli was still reading, he peaked into the top drawer under the boxes. He found a box of envelopes with a lighter inside. There were no stamps inside it.

"Shit," Mrs. Calli said. She rushed up as fast as her body would allow and went to turn off the water. Her bare feet slapped the water along her way to the sink and back to the table. "Oh well. Needed to mop the floor, too."

"Everything alright, Mrs. Calli?"

"Everything's just fine. My daughter is coming to see me, today."

"That's good. Why don't you use your chair to get around? Wouldn't want you to slip in the wet floor. Where's your chair?"

"Haven't you been listening? I don't have time to sit. I've gotta tidy up before my daughter gets here. You just do whatever it is you're supposed to do and leave me alone. I liked the other one better. Where is here?" Mrs. Calli stomped her wet foot down into the puddle.

"Jake isn't with me today, Mrs. Calli."

"Well is he coming back?"

Richard turned and went through the living room, down the hall, past the bathroom, and into the back bedroom.

Mrs. Calli's bedroom was the cleanest of the carpeted rooms in the house. Her chair was too far from the bed for her to get in it without getting up this morning. He pushed the controls to see if the chair had been charged. While he was in here, he checked on the oxygen levels in the tanks by her bed and then rode her chair back through the hall and into the living room.

"Do you know my favorite poem?" Mrs. Calli said.

"What?" Richard got up out of the chair. Mrs. Calli was hand washing her coffee cup and coffee pot in the sink, swallowed by suds up to her neck.

"I said do you know my favorite poem?"

"No, Mrs. Calli."

Mrs. Calli rolled her eyes and continued washing for a few moments. Then she recited.

"There was never a sound beside the wood but one, and that was my long scythe whispering to the ground. What was it it whispered? I know not well myself; Perhaps it was something, perhaps about the lack of sound--" She raised her hands up out of the dishwater. "And that's why it whispered and did not speak. I forget the rest," she said.

"Who wrote that?"

"Walt Whitman. No, Frost. It's in the book here." She flung some soap towards the thick book on the kitchen table. Richard went over to the table, but turned toward a drawer in a stand under the island. "My daughter teaches him at Cornell. Teaches his poems to students, you know. She's a teacher. Has been for years. It's what keeps her so busy. Being in Ithaca would make it hard to come back here. I flew there once. It was beautiful, but the people got too close. I need my space. Never did like to be touched or breathed on or looked at too hard. I could get over all of it except for the space. Need my space. That's something you don't get over if you don't want to." And with a slap of her foot into the puddle under her feet, she slipped. She fell as slow as she walked, slow enough for Richard to grab her and prop her back up by pressing carefully on her shoulders.

"You alright, Mrs. Calli?"

She put her hands up in front of her face.

"Don't you mention a word of that to Amy."

"I won't if you get in your chair, at least until I can get this floor dried up."

She twirled her head and moved her mouth once or twice as she stepped around the island and plopped down into the chair. Her knees pointed up out of the chair when she placed her feet in the footrest.

"Do you have a mop, Mrs. Calli?" Richard asked. Mrs. Calli shook her head and looked up to the dusty ceiling fan over the table in the kitchen, hovering her hands over the arm rests of her chair.

"What do you think this is, a Winn-Dixie? Use a damn towel. There behind you." Richard turned to a thin dish towel behind him. He snatched it off the oven door handle and dropped it over the suds and water. He sloshed it around with his foot over the water, spilling the soap suds from their cluster and allowing the mess to tumble under the table as the water carried it. "Might need a bigger towel."

"Not a problem, Mrs. Calli. Read your book and I'll be right back." Richard sloshed through the suds, stomping hard through the carpet in the living room with his shoes as he went into the hall. Mrs. Calli kept her towels in the closet between the hot water heater and the laundry doors, all of them white, most of them with at least a fleck or two of something black and gray on them.

His cell phone vibrated.

He put the two towels back down.

He said Jake under his breath.

It was only his brother, needing to borrow his glue-gun. He text back that it was in his kitchen, in the bottom drawer nearest the trashcan, and that the back door was unlocked. He stared back at the where-are-you he'd sent Jake that morning for a few moments before putting his phone back in his pocket.

He went into the bathroom and ran his hand down into the top drawer nearest the light switch, sighed, and closed the drawer. He brought the towels into the kitchen. He dropped them on the floor and moved them over the mess with his right foot, bending his knee out and back, ending with a twirl against the table. Mrs. Calli had her chair moved up against the table, her nose in her book.

Richard took out the garbage. He let the green lid close over it. His eyes followed the construction marks on the sidewalk and road back towards his own apartment. Mrs. Calli's poem came to mind. Something perhaps, about the lack of sound, and he forgot the rest. It didn't look like Jake had returned with the vehicle, yet. As his eyes came back to the mark pointing toward him, he turned back around.

The clock between the windows in Mrs. Calli's living room said twelve o'clock, but it was probably wrong. He would be late for his other clients. He could only hope that Jake was already at Mr. Perry's place on Cumberland Avenue.

"Are you ready for lunch?" Richard said. Mrs. Calli grunted and nodded.

"I was going to put the big lasagna on for when my daughter gets here." Richard stepped over to the freezer and dug through the assortment of small frozen meal boxes until he found a large lasagna box. He went to the drawer under the microwave and pulled out a blunt knife, cut a slit in the center of the plastic cover, and put it in the microwave for fifteen minutes.

"It'll be ready in no time. Anything else you need today, Mrs. Calli?"

"Oh, the letter."

"Right, I've got your letter." Richard was already on his way back to the chest of drawers in the living room. He looked at the name on the envelope as he picked it up and checked the return address. He couldn't read her handwriting. He stood in front of the chest of drawers for a few minutes, looking around inside drawers and boxes, and looked under magazines on the coffee table. He sighed as he put the envelope in his pants pocket. He went back into the bedroom one last time to check the gauges on the tanks.

A large box with packages of stamps and envelopes was on an end table near where the chair had been parked. Richard stamped the envelope and dug his hand into the box until he found a small bag of weed at the bottom.

He sneaked into the living room until he saw Mrs. Calli, already standing up again, back at the sink. The water was still off. The microwave was still going.

He grabbed the lighter out of the box from the chest and walked just as carefully back into the bedroom as he came out. He sat on the end of Mrs. Calli's bed and rolled one. The smell of the lasagna lingered from the kitchen as he puffed. He listened to the sounds of Mrs. Calli scuffling and moving, the squeak of the damp floor under her feet, the microwave roaring. The light in the room fell. He cracked the window opposite the bed.

In the kitchen, Mrs. Calli was sitting back in her chair in front of the microwave, watching the lasagna spin. When it stopped, Richard took it out and cut her a square. He put it on a round white plate from above the countertop.

"Is there anything else you need, Mrs. Calli?" She wiggled her lips and waved him away without looking back. "I'll see you tomorrow, Mrs. Calli."

"Don't forget your other half tomorrow. Jake, is it?"

Richard pushed open the screen door. He waited for the screen door to shut before he walked down the steps.

The sun was high. The lines, circles, and dots on the sidewalk were brighter and more colorful as he went past Mrs. Calli's home and on down Lee street. He pulled his phone from his pocket, found no new messages, and sent none before putting it back. He walked slower than he should have.

He looked down. The lines and circles were pointing the way, the lines orange, the dots red, the arrows pink and soft.

He walked on and then he forgot the rest.

Fake Horse Rider

My name's Wess Black, but my friends in college call me Bliss. I ride horses, the plastic kind, in Big Mall on the Maryland side of 495. There's this horsey trail ride that goes all around the inside of the mall. I think it used to be a train ride. Moms put their kids on the horses when they go Christmas shopping. I ride the front horse and I'm supposed to say cowboy things. My professor says it's a character-building job.

I was on the front horse admiring this beautiful girl who worked in the Hot-Hot Pickles in the front of the food court when this kid came into the mall, his thumbs in his blue jean pockets, rocking his head as he walked through the main lobby around the Christmas tree. He looked like he was about six or seven. He's been on the horses before. He always had this yo-yo that he pulled from his pocket and held close.

He grabbed ahold of the mane on the horse behind me and pulled himself up onto the plastic saddle with one hand. I waited for the mall Santa to walk out of the movie theater in front of the food court and flipped the stick on my horse that made it go.

"Yee-Haw", I said. The kid laughed though his nose or his throat, or something, and hocked up a loogie. He spit in the floor.

"Rainbow," the kid said. His throat cleared and the pitch of his laugh rose. He scratched his red hair.

"Watch it, kid," I said. I didn't slow the horses down as they went over the crack under the track before the snowflake gift card ad on the inside of the window at the FYE.

"Fuck you, cocksucker," the kid said.

"Do you even know what that means?" I asked. The kid hopped off the horse and went into the FYE. I rode my horse on around the smaller Christmas tree and fake presents by the JC Penny and on by the North Pole set up past the jewelry store. I looked for the girl when I got back to the Hot-Hot Pickles. She wasn't there. The clock on the screen inside the movie theater said it was eight o'clock. My cell phone buzzed. The time on my phone said it was ten after eight. I had a text message from Boss. If I was still there, I was to come by his office.

Boss's office was down the hallway at the front of the mall with the energy drink machines. He had his office chair facing the window behind his desk. He spun it around and wheeled it over to the other side of his desk while he held a spatula in his hand when I came to the bookshelf with the bookend of a little money playing a drum set. The monkey-shaped bookend held up a collection of white cookbooks with yellow pages. The monkey hollered and beat the drums when I walked past. Boss had a red binder laid out across his desk. It looked like inventory log sheets, like the ones they used in the diner I worked at back home in Louisville. Boss had mostly scribbled in blue ink some one digit numbers beside some words that I couldn't make out from my side of the desk. I smelled the grease on the electric skillet in the windowsill behind him.

"Still a large, Bliss?" Boss asked. He kicked a box out from under the desk at me. There were red long-sleeved shirts inside. They said Free Rides in big white letters. "Iron it before you come in tomorrow." He rolled his gray office chair back over to the window and put three strips of bacon down on the skillet. He asked me if I wanted a sandwich and cracked the window. I said no and put my red shirt on over my old black one to free my hands for the thirty-minute bike ride home.

There was a late-rent notice on my front door and it was still there when I left to go to my Sexuality Identity class the next morning. My professor showed a documentary about the ancient Greek armies and how a lot of the men were in bi-sexual relationships. After class, my professor told me that she didn't have my paper and that I was in danger of failing because I had a D. I told her that I was sorry I forgot about the paper. I told her I had a weird work schedule that week. She said that I showed good character and that I could still turn in the paper for a letter grade lower.

When I got to work at four, Boss was smoking out by the entrance. I went inside as he put out his cigarette.

"Your shirt's wrinkled," Boss said as we walked past the Christmas tree. I clocked in at the end of the energy drink machine hallway and he went into his office. He left his door open. He melted some butter on the electric skillet in the window. I could smell the bacon in the trash by his desk. "Get a new shirt," he said when the monkey smacked the drums. With a spatula in his hand, he pointed his bowed pinky down at the box below his desk. He cracked an egg into the skillet.

"No more larges," I said.

"Watch my egg." He left the office. The monkey didn't make a sound. The binder on his desk was open. Numbers were next to food items: bacon, sausage, a carton of eggs, a gallon of milk. When his egg popped, I flipped it with the spatula. The yolk busted.

Boss came back with an iron and plugged it in. He made me take off my shirt. I watched his egg while the iron heated up. I put the egg on the plate he had next to the skillet.

Boss ironed around the words on the front of the shirt and handed it over the desk to me.

"Want an egg?" He asked.

I declined and walked past the monkey. It hollered and beat the drums. Boss reminded me to iron my shirt when I came back in Friday.

I went over to the horses to saddle up. The horses were parked at the track between the hallway with the energy drink machines and the movie theater in front of the food court. I checked the wheels and wiped the backs of the horses off with a rag and a blue bottle of surface cleaner from the closet in the hallway.

The wheels on the middle horse scraped the track when I started the horses up. The kids walking towards the North Pole all looked. I gave it until the ride passed the food court and then I hopped off. Boss came up behind me with the red binder. "We wanna stay on the horses, Bliss." He high fived the kids watching.

It took a few good kicks and the horses started gliding around the mall quietly again. Boss went back into his office with a tray of fried pickles. Jingle Bell Rock came on. The hot girl came in through the front doors of the mall and I slowed the ride down with the other stick on my horse as slow as it would go. The shine on her shoulder length black hair matched the shine on her black purse. As she walked on back past the

Hot-Hot Pickles sign, a mom brought a little girl over to the horses.

"You wanna ride the ponies, sweetie?"

The little girl had a big nose just like her mom. The mom plopped the little girl onto the middle horse. She pinched the girl's face until the girl crossed her eyes. The mom looked at me and waited until I gave her a nod before she said she'd be back and went on around towards JC Penny. The little girl crossed her arms. We rode on around past the FYE, past the JC Penny, and past the jewelry store. The little girl didn't smile when she saw Santa and the elves at the North Pole taking pictures.

When we came back around to the food court, my girl at Hot-Hot Pickles smiled and said hello to the kid with the yo-yo from yesterday. She gave the kid a sample of fried pickles. He turned around and bumped his head against the red order-line rope. One of the brass poles fell over. My girl came around and picked it up. I could see the kid's smirk from the entrance to the movie theater. The kid flipped me the bird when her butt was in the air. She stood up and he turned his cute face back on before he walked towards the horses. He clutched the square pickle box so tight that it took the shape of a triangle. He held the yo-yo in his other hand. I stepped off my horse and went to Hot-Hot Pickles. My girl aligned the order-line ropes.

"Hi," I said. She turned around. Her name tag said Christina.

"Hello. One minute." She went back around the counter and to the register. "What do you want?"

"No, I work here. Well not here, but over there." I pointed to the little girl on the middle horse chewing her pinky.

"Oh, the pony rides?" There was something about how she said her p's, like she didn't know what to do with them.

"Horses," I said. The skin on the side of my girl's neck wiggled as she smiled. "I just thought you needed help with the poles."

"No, thank you."

I turned away and caught up with the horses on the track. The little girl's arms were crossed again. The mean kid was on the front horse. He was eating his pickles, riding hands free, the string of his yo-yo wrapped around the middle finger of the hand holding the box of pickles. The body of the yo-yo dragged on the floor just shy of the fourth horse. I walked along the side of the track.

"Get off my horse."

"No."

"What's your name, Kid?"

"Bartholomew."

"You might wanna start going by Bart if you ever

wanna get a girlfriend."

"But my name's Bartholomew. What's your name?"

"Bliss."

"Rainbow suits you better."

"I'm not a faggot."

"How come you don't have a girlfriend?"

"You have one?"

"I will." The kid looked back at the food court as it disappeared around the corner behind a holiday family gift discount sign on the FYE window. He hopped off the horse and went inside the FYE. I got back on the horse long enough for Boss to pass me as he ran with security down through the JC Penny. I hopped off and dug through the holiday bargain bin inside FYE until I found a cut-open copy of The Santa Clause 2. The disc was gone. I peeled off the magnetic strip and threw it onto Bartholomew's shirt as he was mashing onto some buttons on an Xbox controller that hung on the wall. I heard the alarm go off as I took the little girl with her arms crossed on around past the North Pole. I smiled when Boss turned back around with security and Rockin Around The Christmas Tree came on.

At eight o'clock I parked the horses between the hallway and the movie theater, watched my girl leave with a candy cane, and clocked out on the time clock in the back of the energy drink machine hallway near Boss's office. I was off the work schedule for two days.

I went to my Sexuality Identity class. She didn't say anything about me not having my paper. My paycheck deposited at midnight. I was still two hundred dollars short on rent. I left the late-rent notice that said happy holidays on the door when I went back to work at four on Friday.

Boss was outside the mall, smoking. He shook his head at me and pointed at the door. He followed me back to his office. The bacon in the trash can was the only thing that made the smell in the room tolerable. Boss plugged in the iron. He fried an omelet. When the iron got hot, I pressed the iron over my shirt and burned off the last three letters in "free". Boss just shook his head. The monkey hollered and beat the drums on my way out.

I cleaned and kicked the horses smooth sailing again. There were parents and kids backed up from the North Pole all the way to the movie theater waiting for pictures with Santa. Kids were on the horses all day. At six-thirty, after Santa went into the movie theater with one of the elves, a bottle of bourbon sticking out of his Santa-suit pocket, this soccer mom posse filled me up with two kids per horse. A boy and a girl were on the horse behind mine, twins in the middle, two boys on the fourth and two slightly older girls on the back. The kids were loud, but they weren't saying anything. The soccer moms smelled like they'd spent two hours trying on samples of perfume at JC Penny. I was glad to smell the salted batter when I passed Hot-Hot Pickles. My girl was by herself behind the register. The line was backed up around the order line ropes and on around the nearest table.

Bartholomew came in through the food court entrance of the mall in his blue jeans and plaid shirt. This time he wore sunglasses. He pulled out ten bucks from his pocket and walked with his arms swaying while he strutted his stuff up to the ordering line at Hot-Hot Pickles. I went on around and collected more kids at the North Pole. When I got back around to the food court, Bartholomew had only moved up a few spaces. It took another ride around until he made it to the register and pointed at dipping sauces. My girl handed them over the counter to him.

I hopped off from my horse and walked over to the ordering line. I got behind a tall man in a real cowboy hat and boots. He had a briefcase in one hand and a bag from the jewelry store in the other.

"Nobody deserves to be left alone like that," the real cowboy said.

"Especially her," I said. The real cowboy turned around. His eyes were brown. His belt buckle said Cole.

"The jewelry store. That's where I got the buckle," he said. He twisted it in the light.

When it was the real cowboy's turn to order, he got a

small box of pickles and a Dr. Pepper. The dipping sauces were extra. He bought two. I kept my hands in my pockets and stared at the real cowboy's belt to keep from looking up at the menu. The real cowboy signed a receipt and dropped an ink pen back down into the clear plastic cup. He stepped aside.

My girl didn't greet me. She wore a red t-shirt under her nametag and a denim skirt. Her hair was as black as ever. She had a silver chain necklace on. It fell over her shoulders and hid down her cleavage. After I studied her nametag, I grabbed the pen from the water cup, and a napkin from the stand.

"Can I have your number, Christina?" Her blue contacts didn't disappear under her eyelids for the whole chorus of Santa Claus Is Coming To Town. Her lips were apart; her top lip curved slightly. She held them there like that. I held the pen and the napkin over the counter.

"No," she said. I had to look away from the silver shine of her necklace. It was the first time I ever wanted to look away. I walked over to the nearest table and scribbled down a phone number. I drew a heart but messed up the corner when the pen fell down into a chip on the end of the table. The real cowboy raised his Dr. Pepper up off the table to me.

I walked back to the track and followed it around to the North Pole. Bartholomew was on the front horse.

"Get off my horse."

"No way, Rainbow."

I held the napkin up to his face. I took it back before he could snatch it and then I flipped him the bird. I think I made him cry. He threw the end of his yo-yo at me. It hit my jaw. I grabbed and yanked the yo-yo and he fell off the horse and onto the floor. Some kids laughed at him as he ran out of the mall. I threw the napkin in the trash by the hallway with the energy drink machines and walked along the track beside the horses. Boss came out of the hallway.

"You have to ride the horses," Boss said.

"I don't give a fuck." I pulled the front of my F Rides shirt away from my chest with my thumbs and index fingers. He pointed to his office and pulled out his walkie. He made an announcement for the moms to come get their kids off the horses.

After the monkey hollered and beat the drums, Boss said he was going to have to let me go. He made me take off my shirt and hat. He asked me if I wanted an egg and bacon sandwich on Texas toast. I said no and he emptied the plate into the trash by the desk. Traffic out the window looked terrible. Boss said merry Christmas, wished me the best of luck, and I left. He yelled after me for the cowboy hat. I took it off and handed it to him in the hallway. On my way back to my bike I thought about Christina and Bartholomew. The real cowboy tapped me on the shoulder by the bike rack.

"I'll bet if you ask her again, she'll say yes," the real cowboy said.

"I don't think it's gonna work out," I said. The real cowboy laughed.

"You remind me of my son." He got in his truck and drove away. I let the thought cross my mind that one day, maybe, if the girl was right, and as long as the kid was nothing like Bartholomew, I might want to have a kid when I become a real cowboy.

A Spaceship

It was the third weekend in a row that Jason hadn't been in the dorm for their weekly gaming night when Tommy started to realize that something wasn't right. After everyone left, Jason slipped in sometime after midnight again. He kicked his shoes off at the door and hung up his red hoodie beside Tommy's blue. Tommy saw his teammate Colin through the crack of the door as Jason came in. Jason's presence continued to dwindle from the group as the weeks passed.

"Where the hell you been?" Tommy said one night, turning on the Xbox. Tommy heard a pause in Jason's pen scratches. Jason was scribbling all over one of Tommy's essays for him.

"I'm the editor of the campus newspaper now," Jason said. Tommy paused his game.

"Oh cool. The hell? You didn't say anything?"

"It's, like, all over the website. Here."

Tommy's essay glided over onto his bed. Jason put it in his underwear drawer.

Tommy turned off the game. He pulled his shirt off, threw it towards the pile of the rest of his clothes, and climbed into bed.

Jason flipped the light.

Tommy unbuttoned his pants under his blanket and kicked them over the end of the bed.

"Tommy?"

"Hmm?" Tommy's eyes closed, and then he woke up the next morning. Jason's bed was already empty.

After midterms, Tommy woke up just in the nick of time to catch Jason as he was sneaking out a little after two o'clock in the morning. Tommy kept his distance and followed him to two floors above. He waited a few hallway turns back from Colin's door. About an hour passed until he saw Jason running around the corner. Tommy flipped his blue hood up and Jason darted past him. He followed the back of Jason's red hoodie for another thirty minutes, out through the back end of campus and into a wooded area off to the side of the onramp to I-65. Through the thick trees, the red hoodie got away from him.

Tommy came to a large clearing surrounded by trees. Through the spaces in between the bark, Tommy saw a red hoodie sitting alone on the edge of a pond in the middle. Jason's messy hair sifted through a breeze as he stared into the water, alone.

"You okay?" Tommy asked after he felt like he'd waited long enough. Jason wiped his face quickly; his skin was as wet as the pond ahead. Under the moonlight, Tommy could see that Jason's face was not quite right.

"Hey," Jason said. Tommy walked closer and examined Jason's face; he could see a faint dark blue blemish just below Jason's left eye.

"What happened?" He reached his hand towards the bruise. Jason pulled his head back. Tommy began to notice the beat of his own heart as he watched the tears rain down from Jason's eyes.

"Colin."

"When?"

"Don't." Jason stood up, his eyes still leaking.

Tommy didn't realize that his hand had fallen down Jason's backside until after Jason had started sobbing again. Jason's tears stained Tommy's white t-shirt. Jason's lips touched Tommy's. Tommy let them stay there for a bit. Tommy felt the air in Jason's lungs seep into his own mouth. Their tongues met a few moments later. Tommy withdrew his lips.

"I'm not gay, Jason."

"Oh." Jason blinked a few times and then rubbed his eyes, and then he stared at something in the water. Tommy squinted his eyes to see through the murk. He could just barely make out a large black round rock resting below. Sweat had started to clamp the tear-stained shirt to Tommy's skin. He pulled it over his head and tossed it behind him. "What are you doing?" Jason asked. Tommy backed away from the water and lunged forward into the pond. He forced his eyes open under the water, but it wasn't clear enough to see the rock. He heard Jason dive in above. Tommy couldn't resist the urge to grab Jason's leg from below and listen to him scream like a girl. He had to bob his head up out of the water to keep from drowning himself with laughter. "This water is warm," Jason said after a few minutes.

"You piss in it?" Tommy asked. Jason rolled his eyes. Jason splashed, then swam to the other side. He stayed there, tugging on the roots and the grass that hung over from the edge. "How deep you think this goes?"

"I don't know." Jason floated on his back, occasionally lifting his hand to his eye. After they climbed up out of the water and dried off with their shirts, Jason glanced back at the rock towards the bottom of the water. "I think it looks like a spaceship."

"It's just a rock," Tommy said as he slipped his shirt back on. They turned and walked back towards their dorm.

"I'm sorry."

"Don't worry about it."

*

The leaves had begun to fall from the trees, and the pond wore them like an autumn scarf with splotches of reds and yellows over a dark blue top. Tommy looked around. He saw a splash. Jason climbed up out of the water holding his shorts around his waist so that the pond couldn't pull them down around his ankles. Tommy sat down Jason's red hoodie and took off his own, then he tossed Jason a tuna sandwich from the food court deli and a beer. They sat and ate. They watched the sun.

"It's just a fucking rock," Tommy said.

"It's clearly a spaceship. I mean, just look at it," Jason said.

"Why would it be here?"

"If you don't think it's a spaceship, why do you even keep coming out here? You trying to catch me skinny dipping?" Tommy gave him a look. "I was just kidding."

"You shouldn't swim in the water by yourself. It's deep."

"Fine." Jason's sandwich was half mashed into his mouth. Tommy tossed him another Keystone Light and opened another for himself.

"What would you do if it was a spaceship?" Tommy

asked. Jason brushed the crumbs from his mouth and picked up a leaf to wipe his hands.

"Fly it. You could come, too."

"It's too small."

After they were done eating, Tommy pulled off his shirt, stepped up to the water, and unzipped his jeans, letting them fall over the grass. He stepped into the water. Jason kept his distance.

Tommy looked at the rock as he soaked in the warmth of water around his thighs and lower back. He tried over and over again to see anything else besides a rock in the bottom of the water, but all that was there was a black rock.

Tommy walked to the pond on a cold night. Jason was supposed to meet him earlier at the food court before the dorms closed, but he never showed. When Tommy got to the clearing, he looked around. There was no sign of Jason. Tommy walked over and stood at the edge of the pond.

Tommy sat by the edge of the water. He watched dragonflies and water striders straddle their long, skinny legs over the surface of the pond.

There was something different about the water.

Tommy examined it as close as he could without falling in. He could no longer feel the warm steam from the water against his face. The pond had gone cold. The water was so crystal-clear now that he could see through it like glass. The rock wasn't there. Tommy dove into the water. He forced his eyes open as he turned his head every which way. He popped his head up for air and swam back down. He looked for the rock until he eyes started to burn. He climbed out of the pond and dried his face with his blue hoodie, pressing the cloth against his eyes. Tommy tilted his head up to the sky. There were no stars to gaze at; it was a cloudy night. Tommy started shivering in his damp clothes. He took off his shirt and looked around the clearing one last time as he made his way back towards campus, stepping over a rusted beer can. He turned and gave the water one last look.

Author Bio

Eric Shay Howard lives in Louisville, Kentucky. He has a Bachelor of Arts from the University of Louisville and edits the literary magazine *Likely Red*.

Made in the USA
Columbia, SC
09 November 2020

24209090R00071